The Show Must Go On

The Show Must Go On

Tina Wells

with Stephanie Smith

Random House New York

This is a work of fiction. Names, characters, places, and incidents either are the product of the author's imagination or are used fictitiously. Any resemblance to actual persons, living or dead, events, or locales is entirely coincidental.

Cover art and interior illustrations by Brittney Bond

 Published in the United States by Random House Children's Books, a division of Penguin Random House LLC, New York.

Random House and the colophon are registered trademarks of Penguin Random House LLC.

Visit us on the Web! rhcbooks.com

Educators and librarians, for a variety of teaching tools, visit us at RHTeachersLibrarians.com

Library of Congress Cataloging-in-Publication Data is available upon request.
ISBN 978-0-593-37927-1 (trade) — ISBN 978-0-593-37893-9 (ebook)

Printed in the United States of America
10 9 8 7 6 5 4 3 2 1
First Edition

For my nephew Maxwell

CHAPTER ONE

Bikes. Park. Noon? the text message from Lee said.

Lee Noel and I have had some of our best times together on bike rides. We've ranked the best movies and music videos of all time. We've talked about where we go when we die. We've made drive-by scavenger hunts that have taken us through our entire subdivision. So of course when he asked me to go for a bike ride on Saturday, the day when I had no field hockey practice and no major tests to study for, I thought that we could spend hours talking and riding. Then maybe he'd ask me to sit on a bench and he'd sit next to me, nervously, and he'd hand me a flower he'd picked from by the river and say that the flower was just as beautiful as I am. And then he'd confess his true feelings for me and ask that we get married when we're older and raise our family near our parents and grandparents in Featherstone Creek. Or we'd just ride bikes. Whatever.

Yeah, sure 👍, I answered, eager to hang out with him, but wondered if something was up.

At least I knew one thing for sure: *I think Lee is someone special. But no one knows that.*

Lee and I had been close friends for years. But lately, I'd felt our relationship was changing. We were getting older, more mature, and it felt like our friendship was also moving in that direction. We were having more in-depth talks about the future, the world. He'd been asking to come to Sunday dinner every week. Yes, my mother's cooking was good. But was he *really* just there for the food?

The truth of the matter here was that Lee was my best guy friend who I'd started to see as more than just a friend. But if I told him that, a few things could happen. One, he could confess he feels the same way. Or two—gasp, ugh, ack!—he could say "I like you, but I don't *like you* like you." And then things would be different. He wouldn't come over for Sunday dinner anymore, he wouldn't text me funny videos of squirrels twerking, we wouldn't ride bikes together, and we wouldn't go to our lake houses together and hang out all day. The potential for option two to happen was enough to make me want to keep my mouth shut.

And I couldn't just ask him directly if he felt the same way. That would automatically make things weird. I couldn't say what I was feeling, either. I didn't exactly understand what I was feeling. I was only eleven years old! I was hardly an expert on relationships yet. Besides that, I had other issues—things that were weighing much more heavily on me than just a potential crush on my best guy friend.

The heaviest thing on my mind is this: I can only tell the truth. About everything. About the weather, my grades, my preference for chicken over steak, and, of course, who I might have a crush on. And this predicament, or superpower, depending on who you ask, is all thanks to one woman. *Victoria*.

I met Victoria a couple of months ago, at the fun house at the Featherstone Creek Festival. She claimed to be a fairy godmother, and she put a spell on me that makes me tell the truth. I literally cannot lie. When I try to lie, she gives me signals that she's watching

and that I need to be honest with people. Say I'm talking about how I don't like asparagus, even though I really do. All of a sudden, I'll get hit with a sneeze attack. It's like Victoria has sprinkled pepper all over my lunch. The only way to get it to stop is to confess that I really do like asparagus. In other words, tell the truth. In fact, the only way she'll lift the spell entirely is if I tell the truth entirely. To everyone. No matter what.

I've tried to hold back truths that would hurt people, or at least not say them out loud so that other people could hear them and possibly be hurt. I like making people happy. I get joy out of seeing others happy. So instead I write my truths down in a secret blog, to keep people's feelings from being hurt. Which has worked—whenever I have to confess something embarrassing or something that's not ideal about myself or anyone else, I write it down before it comes spewing out of my mouth.

In some ways, it's been a blessing. Since I've been telling people my honest opinions out loud to their faces, I've been doing fewer things to make other people happy and more things that I want to do. Following my own passions, like writing for the school newspaper. Picking out my own clothes.

In other ways, it's been a curse. I told my dad that I didn't necessarily want to be a lawyer like he is, and it didn't go over too well. Granted, I told him by making a scene at a restaurant, like a baby having a temper tantrum. I really gotta work on my delivery.

With all truths, there are consequences. Some are good—admitting you're lost and need directions, then getting those directions and finding your way. Or admitting you can't do something, and having someone teach you how. Some truths cause disagreements. For example, I like pears and someone else doesn't, and now we have to end up debating which fruit makes for a better snack.

But the hardest consequence to deal with is rejection. Someone saying your hopes and dreams are never happening. Someone saying you can't do what you want to do. Someone out there trying to prevent you from living that truth.

So with all that uncertainty, all that potential for disaster, what would you do?

In my case, I have to tell the truth, of course. No matter what it costs me.

Unless it's about Lee. That's a truth I'm not ready to let out yet.

CHAPTER TWO

I put on my favorite sweatpants and hoodie over a white T-shirt and pulled my hair back into a bun. I jammed my feet into my white slip-ons and walked toward the garage to grab my bike. When I opened the garage door, Lee was already in my driveway, pulling up to my house wearing a flannel shirt and jeans. And Timberlands.

"Timbs to go bike riding?"

"We'll be by the river," he said. "It could get muddy."

"Right . . . ," I said, looking down at my white shoes. "These won't work, then." Leave it to Lee to be spontaneous and not tell me the plan ahead of time.

I went back inside to the mudroom to change them out for my older black Nike high-tops. "All right," I said, walking back toward my bike, feeling even more uneasy

about what was in store for me and Lee. What were we going to do by the river? Were things about to get messy? "Let's head out."

We rode side by side down our street to the main road that took us toward the park. I let Lee take the lead as I admired the leaves hanging above the road—they'd already begun to change colors, and I found a rainbow of reds and browns along the edges of the sidewalks. I looked at Lee from behind. Did he get, like, two inches taller since last time I saw him?

We hung a right and headed toward the park at the base of the river, where families had gathered to watch the geese dance around the lake and kids took turns on the slide and the swings. The weather was still warm enough on this November Saturday to only need a light jacket, and the snack cart that sold coffee and ice cream was still open, even this late in the season. "The park's hopping today," I said. "Remember how many times I've fallen on those monkey bars? I almost broke my arm once!"

"Once?" Lee said. "Maybe a few more times than that!"

We pedaled our bikes toward the river path, and then dismounted and started walking them toward the creek. "So, what's up?" he asked me.

What's up, he asks. Hah! Well, the truth is, in addition to trying to make my mark as a sixth grader at Featherstone Creek Middle School, including being the next great field hockey all-American and a Pulitzer Prize–winning journalist for the school newspaper, I'd been desperately trying to craft an escape from this God-blessed truth-telling curse. It had come *this close* to ruining my life these past couple of months. But I couldn't tell him all of this . . . and I couldn't lie. I'd give him the short version.

"You know, school, field hockey, the usual. What's up with you?" I responded.

"You know, school, grandparents . . . Mom and Dad sent me another package the other day. Apparently, they're trying to come back for the holidays." Lee's parents were in the military and currently stationed somewhere in the Pacific Ocean. While they'd been gone, Lee had lived with his grandparents for the past five years.

"So, uh," he continued, "what's up with your girl Nia? You see her lately?"

"No," I replied. "I just got off punishment, so now that I'm free again, I've been trying to focus on school. Not so much time for hanging out."

"I feel you," Lee said. "But she's your best friend, isn't she?"

"Yeah, it's just . . ." I was aware that Victoria was watching me. She's always watching me, fact-checking my every word. If I lied, she would remind me to change my tune—her fairy dust sent me into an unavoidable sneezing fit. I liked to avoid the excessive achoo-ing if possible.

"I just . . . I needed to get my ducks in a row for school. Haven't had the time."

"Ah, cool," he said, looking down at the front wheel of his bike. Was he . . . *nervous*? "So now that you're free, maybe we should ask her to hang out with us sometime?"

I looked at him, searching for the real meaning behind his request. While we've all been friends since we were little, it was sort of understood that Lee was the outdoorsy, dirt-and-grime type of guy, and my bestie Nia Shorter was a fashion-and-beauty-tutorials-on-YouTube type of girl. Lee loved everything about being out in nature—fishing, bugs, mud. Nia did play basketball, and was quite good, so she wasn't that prissy. Still, Nia would rather be at the mall than at the creek.

"What do you mean, 'hang out with us'? Like, all together as a group?"

"Like, yeah," Lee said, a quiver vibrating his voice. "I haven't hung out with her in a while. We were in class the other day and I was, you know, thinking to myself that we should make more of an effort to, like, hang out all together."

I couldn't believe what I was hearing. I couldn't remember the last time Lee went to the mall, and that was Nia's favorite place to hang out. What were he and Nia going to do there? Sit on Santa's lap and take photos? Why did he want to spend more time with Nia?

“Did she ever mention wanting to hang out with me?” Lee asked eagerly.

“I can’t remember,” I said. The truth. Especially because at one point Lee seemed to have totally fallen off Nia’s radar—she was asking about Lee’s best friend, Alvin Abramson, instead. But then she stopped asking about Alvin. Was she interested in someone else altogether? Or had she actually been interested in Lee all along?!

"Wait . . . so you want to hang out with Nia?" I repeated, still dumbfounded.

"I'm saying we don't all kick it, and, like, why not?" Lee defended, shrugging. "You know, she's cool."

"Cool?"

"Yeah, June, cool. Don't you think?"

Cool? I thought to myself. Like *cool* cool? Like cool and pretty cool? Like "cool, I want to be cool with her, too" cool?? My heart sank in my chest. My mouth felt dry. I felt like . . . well, I needed to be direct here . . .

"Are you saying you like her?" I asked Lee outright. I felt a stabbing pain in my chest as I said it out loud. I didn't know if it was gas or jealousy but whatever it was, it was uncomfortable.

"I mean, I don't know if I *like her* like her yet, but I also don't know her that well. And I should get to know her better," he said. "That's all. And who knows? Maybe then I'll like her some more."

Lee had never expressed feelings about another person before in our conversations. I guess I'd thought that because we normally spent so much of our time together, I could be the only person he would have feelings for—he just didn't have time to spend with other girls, between Creek's Club and time with his grandparents.

I looked at him. My chest still hurt and my hands

suddenly felt sweaty, slipping against the handlebars of my bike. I felt a sense of loss. Like my cat had just died. My imaginary cat, that is. I call him Rufus.

I didn't know what to do. This feeling in my chest was something I didn't want to linger for months on end while a possible new relationship between Lee and Nia grew. I had to deflect the situation. Maybe if Lee thought Nia wasn't interested, he would back off? I pivoted.

"Well, I mean, I just don't think that she's ever said anything about you," I said. Which was kind of true. My nose twitched.

"Yeah?" Lee said. "Again, another reason that we should get to know each other better. Spend some time together."

It felt like my eyes were sinking deeper into my face. Did Lee seriously want to date Nia? Because all of us were a bit young for that. Right now, anyway. At least that's what my parents had told me. But my mind jumped to what might happen between Nia and Lee in the future. I pictured them together. Like "boyfriend/girlfriend." Like kissing. I wanted to unsee it.

I just couldn't believe that, without even knowing it, my best friend had taken my crush away from me, right out from under my nose. But she had no idea what she'd done. Because she . . . really didn't do anything. I mean, who knew if Nia even liked him back? Even if they did get together and start dating, maybe she'd end up breaking

his heart and then he'd realize his one true love was me after all?

My thoughts were spiraling and I was starting to feel nauseated. I had to play it cool. Not lie, just be . . . neutral. I couldn't shut the conversation down forever—Lee seemed determined. So I just had to end it for now, and maybe later on I could pretend Lee had never said anything to me about Nia in the first place.

"Okay," I said. "We'll all get together and hang out."

"Yeah, cool. Great. Awesome," Lee said, hopping

back on his bike. He started pedaling around the creek. I stamped my feet onto the pedals and lurched myself forward, following behind him, pushing harder to keep up the pace. Lee liking Nia wouldn't be the worst thing in the world—but it sure did feel like it right now. Should I have told him how I really felt? Would that have changed his mind at all about Nia? Or was I about to lose my crush and my BFF at the same time?

CHAPTER THREE

I got home from the bike ride and immediately went up to my room to sulk. I could barely concentrate on whatever Lee was talking about for the rest of our hangout after he dropped the news about Nia. I mean, of all people to admit he had a crush on . . . ! My best friend! And besides, if Lee was going to be into anyone, I would think he'd be more interested in my other best friend Olive Banks. She's creative, crafty, in orchestra, and doesn't mind getting her hands dirty. But, really, Nia? The girliest girl in town? Really, Lee? I felt so frustrated. And a little sad. And a little . . . gosh, I didn't know. But I had to do something about it, otherwise I was just going to feel worse and worse. So I wrote a few lines in my secret blog:

HONEST June

CONFESSION #20:

I cannot believe this—Lee and Nia? Together? Like, he has a crush on her? When did this happen? In math class? Science? I mean, it's not like they've ever hung out one-on-one. We all just eat together in the cafeteria. And now, what, am I supposed to tell Nia how he feels? I can't just hand over my secret boy crush, the person I wanted to spend my entire life with, to my best friend. She doesn't even like the same things as Lee! Does he know she doesn't like to get her fingernails dirty playing in creek mud? Does he know she doesn't like reptiles? They creep her out. He'll never even be able to take his pet lizard, Chadwick, with them on hangouts, you know. Plus, Lee is one of the nicest, most polite people I've ever known in my life, and Nia—well, she is nice, too, but also can really hurt someone's feelings if they cross her. I just. Can't. Believe. Any of this. 😖

I logged out of my blog and sat back on the bed, slumping my shoulders. Then I picked up my cell phone and dialed the one person who would know what to do in this kind of crisis. I called Chloe Lawrence-Johnson.

"Hey, girl!" Chloe said in a perky voice. "What's up?"

"*Siiiggghh* . . . hi."

"Girl, I can hear the sadness through the phone," Chloe said. "What is wrong?"

"I just . . . I just don't know. . . ." I still didn't know how to explain the Lee-and-Nia situation out loud.

"What, Victoria got you tongue-tied?"

"No," I said. "I just got, like, the worst info. Lee wanted to ride to the park, so we went, and he told me I should invite Nia to hang out with us sometime."

"Nia?" Chloe said. "Okay. What's the big deal?"

"You know, hang out with *us*. So he eventually can 'hang out' with *her. Just* her."

"Ohhhh," Chloe said, finally picking up what I was putting down. "But Lee's, like, 'your' guy, right? Isn't that what you told me?"

"I never said that!" I said. I had never admitted out loud to anyone that I had any feelings for Lee. "Okay, I had, like, one dream about our wedding. But, like, I never said I *liked him* liked him. If anything, *he* was acting like he had a crush on *me*! All those times he comes over for Sunday dinner? All the time we spent together at our lake houses? We had a different kind of friendship! So I thought." I knew it was probably just wishful thinking. . . . I was pretty positive Lee had only ever seen me as a good friend. And now I knew for *sure* he did.

I knew I felt differently about Lee than I did other boys. Like I only blushed when Lee sat close to me. I only laughed my snort laugh when Lee told jokes. Lee is also the only boy I have ever touched a real live frog for. I don't do that for just anyone. And I know Nia wouldn't do that for anyone!

"You know what this means," I continued. "Now he'll only want to hang out with her, and then he'll never hang out with me anymore! Chloe, I don't want to lose him! I don't want to be the third wheel for my two best friends in Featherstone Creek! I gotta figure out how I'm going to steal Lee back from Nia. Which is awful, but it must be done for, like, the greater good!"

"The greater good of *what*? Yourself? Girl, get a grip," Chloe said, chuckling. "First of all, can we talk about the important things?"

"Like what? This is important!"

"No, field hockey is important. Your grades are important. Staying on your parents' good side is important. Do you think you should pay more attention to those things than try to get a boyfriend right now? Didn't you just get off punishment, like, two days ago?"

Chloe was right. Why is she so practical? Dang it!

"And besides, Lee didn't say he wanted to be bf/gf with Nia immediately. He just asked if you would invite her to hang out more. He didn't say he wanted Nia to be his future wife. Or even call her dad and ask for his permission to take her out or anything. Chilllllll."

"I know, but this, like, *changes* things!" I said.

"No, it doesn't. As long as you don't let it, it changes nothing. Relax, girl. It's Saturday. Dang, you bringin' Monday drama here. When are you going to tell Nia?"

Bleuuch!! "Um, do I have to?"

"Um, *yes,* girl, she is your other best friend. You can't hide this from her, especially if Lee wants her to know he's interested, which he does. Maybe she has some feelings for him, too."

That is not a vision I wanted to have in my head. Nia would work her charm on Lee and all of a sudden they'd be bf/gf, just like that. "I don't know. I just don't know if I can do this." I took my hair out of my bun and started braiding it in frustration.

"Well, you have to tell them the truth. Don't sit there and be a roadblock to their budding relationship."

"Thanks, Chloe," I said sarcastically. I ended the call, scrunching up my face in defeat.

Just as I put down the phone and was thinking I could close my eyes and pretend it could all disappear, fairy dust erupted in front of my face. First just a cloud. Then a whole storm of fairy dust, swirling downward from the ceiling in a tornado of sparkles and glitter. The wind whipped through my hair and made my eyes water. Only one person could create this kind of mess.

"June, my dear! It's been a minute," Victoria greeted as she popped into my room at the tail end of the fairy dust storm cloud. One of her slippers had come off her foot, and she reached down to put it back on.

"Only a minute," I said with a groan. "Weren't you just here?"

"A few days ago, dear, but I saw what went down between you and Lee today—and you not telling Lee how you feel about him *and* not telling him the whole truth about Nia. Honey, let's discuss."

"Let's not?"

"You want this spell lifted before you get your driver's license or what?" Victoria said, winking.

"Goodness, okay," I said. "So, what, I'm supposed to tell him I like him *after* he confesses he likes my best friend instead?"

"Well, did he say that? Sounds like he said he wanted to spend more time with the two of you together. Either way, why didn't you tell him that Nia had asked about him, too?"

"Because she only asked once, and I've seen her more curious about a new pair of shoes than about Lee."

"Uh-huh," Victoria said with a roll of her eyes. "You sure? You sure there's not *one* pang of jealousy keeping you from getting on the phone with Nia right now and telling her about your bike ride?"

"But maybe Lee wanted me to keep it a secret," I said, and sniffled because Victoria was 100 percent right.

"You could still ask her to hang out with you and Lee, like he wanted, without mentioning any potential crushes."

None of these options seemed good. I didn't want to tell Lee my true feelings. I didn't want any part of Lee's relationship with anyone else. And a big part of me didn't *want* to help Nia steal away my best guy friend, even if she was my best girl friend! "Can't I just stay out of it?"

"Is that really doing the best service to your friends?" Victoria asked. "I suggest you think about this before you decide to say nothing. Withholding facts is still lying. Remember, you must always tell the truth, to everyone. That's the only way this spell gets lifted. I'm watching you."

And then Victoria took two steps backward, and twirled in a tight counterclockwise circle until a blur of fairy dust and sparkles surrounded her, wrapping her in a tight cone-shaped spiral. Then it released her upward into thin air once again. The pile of fairy dust quickly fell to the ground, right alongside my broken heart—here, finally, was the consequence of realizing my best guy friend didn't have the same mushy feelings about me that I did about him.

CONFESSION #21:

So Lee doesn't like me. Or at least he doesn't like me in that way. *Lee doesn't like me.* I hate how that sounds. It's like admitting tropical punch Kool-Aid tastes like a bunch of old Nerds dissolved in water. Does this mean he'll never like me? Am I not cool enough? Not smart enough? (Remember that C minus on our math quiz earlier this semester! 😳) Am I not fun to hang out with anymore?? I'm fun! I'm funny! But wait—I have to tell the truth all the time! I'm too busy focusing on that to crack jokes. I can't make funny commentary! Maybe I'm not funny anymore! Maybe I'm not even fun to hang out with anymore! SEE, this truth-telling spell is GOING TO RUIN MY LIFE!!!

CHAPTER FOUR

Nia and Olive were waiting for me at the end of my driveway on Monday morning as usual for us to walk to school together. Because the rest of our school schedules were so busy—Olive had orchestra, Nia was gearing up for basketball season, and I was finishing up field hockey season—none of us had much time after school to just hang anymore, like we could in elementary school. We used the morning walks and lunchtime to catch up on our days.

"Hey, girl!" Olive waved and smiled with her entire face, eyes wide, all her teeth showing, like she ate sunshine for breakfast. Nia nodded and smiled as I approached her. Her hair was pulled back away from her face, showing off her smooth brown cheekbones.

"Hey, y'all," I said. I felt that small pang in my chest again, and Lee popped into my mind. *I should tell Nia that Lee asked about her. I know I should. I know. I will. Later.*

We swapped notes about math homework and the social studies reading as we started walking toward school. "I hear our history teacher is going to have us study *Hamilton* next. Have y'all seen it?"

"Of course, girl," Olive said. "I was obsessed when the Broadway show recording came out on Disney+. I wonder what parts we'll have to study."

"I've seen parts. Mainly on YouTube," Nia said. We'd

arrived on campus a few minutes earlier than usual, having walked at a slightly faster pace in the cool fall air. Nia gave her usual greetings to Kenya and Rachelle and anyone else she recognized (practically everyone) on campus. Olive quickly scurried to her locker to sort out her sheet music and store her viola. We reunited in homeroom.

Mrs. Worth got us settled before our principal made a few quick announcements over the intercom: "Okay, guys, hi! Our major announcement for the day is the reveal of the spring school musical. Produced by the theater department, the musical we will be performing is . . . *The Wiz*! Auditions will be held the week after Thanksgiving break. Check the signs posted in the cafeteria for more details."

My eyes widened. I took a big inhale in, then let out the world's loudest, most excited squeal. I looked at Nia. I knew she'd be as excited as I was. I'd only made her watch clips of "Ease on Down the Road" like a hundred times.

"What's *The Wiz*?" someone asked from the back. My neck whipped around.

"What do you mean, what's *The Wiz*? It's only one of the most important pieces of Black American theater of our time!"

"Thought that was *Dreamgirls*," Nia responded.

"Or *Fences*," Olive answered.

"Or *Madea's Family Reunion*," said Eustice from the back.

"Before *all* of those," I said, "there was *The Wiz*. C'mon, guys, with Diana Ross and Michael Jackson? It's a classic!"

I freaking love *The Wiz*. I know, it's perhaps a bit strange that someone my age would even know about it, much less love it. But my parents first showed me the movie when it was on television during the holidays one year, and since then it's become somewhat of a holiday tradition—we watch every year. Mom and Dad know all the songs, and they both end up getting up from the couch at some point during the musical to jam to their favorites. Even my dad—yes, Howard Law Dad—loosens up every time he hears "Don't Nobody Bring Me No Bad News."

The Wiz was coming to Featherstone Creek Middle School. I had to be a part of this.

✦

I tried to concentrate through the rest of my morning classes, but it was near impossible. I kept daydreaming about what part I could possibly play. Maybe a singing and dancing role in the ensemble? A winged monkey? Aunt Em? Glinda, the good witch? Evillene, the bad witch? Or, could I even play Dorothy?! I did know all her lines! My mind swirled with the possibilities.

Nia and Olive were already in the cafeteria when I arrived for lunch after stopping by my locker. The girls gathered at the main counter and loaded their trays full of food and drinks. Nia sat down next to Lee and Alvin, and Olive and I shared the other end of the circular cafeteria table. I unwrapped the yummy sweet-potato-and-turkey wrap with honey mustard my mom made for me from last night's leftovers, which I was eager to dive into. I was even more eager, though, to discuss today's big news.

"Okay, so who's going to audition?" I asked. "Olive, you'll be in the orchestra for the show, right?"

"Um." She took a bite of her sandwich. "Probably. But Mr. Burns didn't mention anything about it in orchestra today."

"Okay, well, maybe he will during your after-school practice. You should totally audition! Nia, any interest?"

"Nope," Nia replied. *Really?!* I thought she'd be as enthusiastic about it as I was!

"Um, why not?" I asked.

"Because it's, like, not my thing," Nia said, not looking up from her meal.

"*The Wiz* is everybody's thing! It's a musical! With Diana Ross and Michael Jackson in it! It's, like, the most fun musical ever!"

"It's still a musical. It's still the theater, June. I don't do theater."

"Say what?" I said.

Nia turned her body toward me. "I'm not an actress. What if I audition, what, they'll make me a Munchkin or a tree or something? That does not sound cool. And then I'll have to deal with the lead actresses from the upper grades and their egos and them thinking they're, like, superior because they're the lead actresses. I do not want to be in a dank theater surrounded by people who think they're the next Lupita Nyong'o when they can't even fake leg cramps good enough to get out of gym class."

"Wow, tell us how you really feel," I said, shocked that something as family friendly as *The Wiz* could cause such disdain in Nia. I mean, she could at least want to audition if it meant we would be Munchkins together.

"June, are you going out for it?" Olive asked.

I thought before I opened my mouth. I didn't want to lie. Really, I couldn't lie because that dreaded Victoria could show up any minute to toss some fairy dust on my turkey wrap and then I'd look like I was having an allergic reaction at lunch and then everyone would freak out and call for a medic to stab me with an EpiPen. Let's avoid that. Plus, I truly hadn't decided what I wanted to do. I wanted to be a part of the production for sure, even if it meant being a Munchkin. But could I audition to be something more? I wanted to be good. I wanted to be great.

I also didn't want to deal with Nia's berating if I did want to go out for a part. Or if I went for a part and didn't get it. What if I wasn't good enough to even be a Munchkin? I didn't want her to call me lame in front of everyone. Especially Lee. My heart began racing.

"I mean," I started to say. "I haven't really decided." That was the truth. "Look, I know I don't have a ton of experience onstage."

Nia looked at me. "Girl, don't you have enough going on with field hockey and the paper and stuff? You can barely keep a date for Sunday dinner in your own house!"

"Field hockey ends next week," I said. "That'll free up some time for the school musical."

Speaking of field hockey, Blake Williams, my good friend and teammate, walked up the row of tables toward me carrying her tray of food and chatting with another girl from the team. I reached out a hand to get her attention. "Hey, girl. You hear about the school play? Are you going to audition?"

"I don't know," Blake said. "I could always be part of the dance crew. I took ballet when I was younger. Now mostly jazz and hip-hop, when I can squeeze it in." She turned toward the cafeteria line. "I'm going to see if there are any tater tots left."

Lee, who I didn't look at this entire lunch for fear I'd accidentally blurt out something about him and Nia, seemed even less interested in the play.

"I can't sing or dance, but maybe I can help build the set or something," he said with a shrug.

I expected Alvin to have even less interest than Lee, since he was more into computers and tech stuff. But he surprised me! "I'm down," he said confidently. "I could be the Scarecrow. I've got the vocals, and I could study Michael Jackson's moves."

I was stunned. Alvin knew how to *sing*? Nia looked up from her sandwich with eyebrows raised.

"What? Just because I can code doesn't mean I can't sing, too," he said. "I've been singing in church since I was three."

"My man can belt out notes like Luther Vandross, Leon Bridges, and John Legend combined," Lee said, giving Alvin a fist bump.

I gave an approving nod. At least I had one buddy in my quest to join *The Wiz*. "Well, then, maybe I could be like the next Diana Ross. Why not?" I said, growing more hopeful by the minute.

Nia turned her back toward her lunch and shook her head—almost as if she wanted to tell me not to do it but didn't want to even make the effort to warn her friend not to make a fool of herself. Then she quickly spoke up, before I could push her any further. "Anyone got notes for next period's history class? If she gives a quiz, I want to be ready."

Everyone turned their attention back to their lunches, and eventually to other things like schoolwork and after-school plans and whatever was trending on TikTok. But my mind was stuck in Oz, daydreaming about the Tin-man, Scarecrow, and Lion, and pondering the important questions about putting together this magical musical. . . . I wonder if we'd get a real dog to play Toto or use a stuffed one?

And the wizards! There's, like, a bunch of wizards and fairy godmothers in that play, including Glinda the Good, Evillene, and the Wizard of Oz himself. Gosh, if anyone knew about fairy godmothers and magical spells, it would be me. They're a tricky bunch, I tell ya.

✦

I looked out the window during class, my mind drifting away from the lesson. I really wanted to be a part of *The Wiz*. But I'd never acted before. The closest acting I'd done was dressing up for Halloween. I was no Ayanna Pullman, who was in seventh grade and had been doing commercials since she was a baby. She even had a manager, and I heard she went to Los Angeles last spring for something called "pilot season." She was a big deal.

Just because I was a girl obsessed with *The Wiz,* that did not make me good enough to play Dorothy. Maybe I was more of a Tinman. Like Nia said, the seventh and eighth graders would probably get all the lead roles. Right? What shot could I have of getting a role that would get me any real stage time? My mind started racing again. Maybe I could do something behind the scenes. Like join the stage crew!

If I auditioned, no matter what role I got—Dorothy, Tinman, a Winkie, or a stage crew hand—I was going to rock it out like my life depended on it. I would do what was best for the production. To make both the cast and the audience happy so we could put on the best possible show. See, I wouldn't even have to lie this time to make people happy! I'd just be doing something that I genuinely liked—might even love, once I had the chance to try it out!

Should I do this? Could I possibly give as great a performance as Diana Ross and Michael Jackson did in the original movie? Could I even hold that legendary note that Diana Ross did in "Home"? Was this a good idea? My head hurt from thinking so hard. I was anxious about just auditioning—how would I feel if I actually got a part and had to perform onstage?

I pulled up the notes app on my computer and weighed the pros and cons.

Pros and cons list for auditioning for *The Wiz*

Pros

Love the play

Know all the words

Get to express my creative side

Blake is doing it too

Mom will be proud (will Dad???)

Cons

Nia thinks it's lame

One more thing to commit to (though field hockey ends in another week or two)

Never acted before—could fail miserably

Never sang in public before—could fail miserably

Could embarrass my whole family and bloodline by failing miserably

Could become laughingstock of school, Featherstone Creek, and all eleven-year-olds of America by failing miserably

Could end all chances of a future, a great career, a stable family life, and a strong social network with an embarrassing performance, thus failing miserably at both the play and at life

I looked at my list. My eyes fixed on the list of cons. The negatives. The possible catastrophes that could happen because of my first crack at acting. *Oh my.* I was chewing the inside of my mouth nervously, and my fingernails beat against the keyboard. I was risking it all by auditioning. Could I really do this? I could confidently say: I had no idea what to do.

HONEST June

CONFESSION #25:

OMG, the most amazing thing happened at school today. We found out the theater department is putting on a production of *The Wiz.* 👠🎬🎼 I want to audition, but none of my friends think it's a good idea. Except for Alvin, who apparently can sing. I have seen the movie a thousand times, but I've never sung in public, onstage, in front of my entire town. And what if I am not that great? What if I can't carry a tune? I mean, is there any chance I could play Dorothy with literally zero acting experience? Maybe I shouldn't go out for it. Maybe Nia was right. . . .

But, hold on. Why is Nia hating? Shouldn't she be encouraging me to go out there and rock it? Shouldn't she be my hype man? My wing girl? My best friend? I'm kinda annoyed she wasn't cheering me on when I mentioned the play. Makes me want to audition just to prove to her I can do it.

CHAPTER FIVE

Nia and Olive wanted to meet up after school. But as tempting as it was, I had other things on my mind. "I can't," I said.

"Why?" Nia asked.

"I have a meeting," I replied. Which was true, but not the whole truth. . . . I did have a school paper meeting—I have them every Monday. But after, I planned to rush home to study every move, every dance, every character of *The Wiz*.

I felt my nose itch. If I didn't tell the truth soon, it would become a full-blown sneeze attack. Victoria always sends a poof of fairy dust even when

I'm thinking about lying to keep me in line. "Okay, okay . . . I want to go home and do some research on *The Wiz*."

Nia raised her eyebrows, then nodded. "Good luck," Nia said. "We'll be at my place if you want to ease on down, ease on down the road."

Even I had to laugh at her fine use of the lyric. "All right. I'll catch up with you later!"

✦

After dinner that night, I settled in to my room, pulled my laptop onto my bed along with a notebook, and got ready for a study session on *The Wiz*.

I pulled up clips from the movie on YouTube. I was immediately taken by the performances. Michael Jackson as Scarecrow. Diana Ross as Dorothy. How she expressed so much through her eyes, with a twirl of her skirt. The music. The costumes—like in the factory when they sing "Don't Nobody Bring Me No Bad News." Wait, is Oz where Victoria was born? I feel like her mother could have been one of these backup dancers or something. Anyway.

And Michael, how could he be so energetic even though he was tied to a pole? I'm sorry, did people actually believe the Scarecrow didn't have a brain? I started singing along to his big solo number—"You can't wiiiin!"—bopping my head from side to side and smiling.

I was shocked this song hadn't been sampled by some trap music producer or hip-hop star and landed on the Billboard charts yet.

I pulled up Diana Ross's big ballad "Home" and watched as she sang with tears in her eyes. Then her voice changed from a sad quaver to determined and focused, and it was a whole vibe. This range of emotion, the expression in their voices. I think this is how the greats, like Bey and Adele and Ariana, learned to perform. I also watched clips of Stephanie Mills, who was the original Dorothy in the Broadway version, because my parents played her version around the house, too.

I took notes as I watched, noting head movements, changes in tone, when to touch certain characters and when to let a note linger longer than the orchestration allowed. I wanted to at least look like I knew what I was doing. Or what I should be doing. I took it seriously. More seriously than my actual schoolwork.

I shut my laptop after nearly two hours of watching clips and taking notes, my head spinning. I headed to the bathroom for a quick shower before I went to bed so I could spend as much time as possible in the morning studying *The Wiz* before school. I also figured I could sing in the shower without anyone hearing me.

"C'mon and ease on down, ease on down the road . . ."

I closed my eyes as the water massaged my shoulders.

The words just flew out of my mouth, my voice getting stronger and louder. My shoulders and my forehead relaxed. For what felt like the first time in months, I was not worrying about school or getting someplace on time or field hockey or studying or what my dad thought about me. And though I did just spend two hours studying all things *The Wiz,* I felt happy. Worry-free. I started bopping my shoulders to the beat in my head, and focused only on the words coming out of my mouth. And it felt *really* good to sing. Like it gave me hope—hope that I could land a role in the play, hope that I could follow my passion, and finally convince Victoria I'd learned enough about telling the truth to lift the curse.

I got out of the shower and toweled off, then reached for some cocoa butter. I kept singing, grabbing a hairbrush and posing dramatically in front of the mirror. I smiled as I saw myself in the mirror. I could make a good Dorothy. Just needed that short Afro. Could I cut my hair? Should I get a wig? I wrapped the towel around myself and let my arms go wide, pretending to bow in front of an imaginary audience.

I opened the door to my bathroom and immediately screamed in fright and clutched the top of my towel. My mother was standing there in the hallway, just outside the door.

"What the . . . geez!" I blurted out.

"Sorry, honey, I didn't mean to scare you!" she said, half chuckling.

"Well, ya did!" I shrieked, my hand at my neck. "What are you doing, stalking me?"

"I can't stalk you in a house I pay the mortgage on," she said. "Was that *The Wiz* you were singing in there?"

Drat. I cringed and shrugged. Guess I was singing loud enough for the whole house to hear me. I wasn't quite yet ready to tell them I wanted to audition for the musical. I hadn't even decided if I was *going* to audition yet. Heck, I didn't even know if I sounded okay. That is, I didn't know if other people thought I sounded okay.

Mom smiled. "June, you sounded really good. I didn't know you could sing!"

"Well, I mean, I was in the shower. Can't most people hold a tune in the bathroom? With the acoustics or whatever?" I adjusted my towel and fidgeted.

"That was more than just holding a tune. You had some spunk and energy in there! And *The Wiz* . . . What made you want to sing that song? Is there nothing new out by Rihanna or Lizzo?"

"Very funny. I just, um, like the song."

"Really?" Mom said, raising an eyebrow.

Suddenly, I felt the urge to sneeze. *Dang it, Victoria, can't I just get dressed first before I tell her the truth?*

I shuffled into my room before I sneezed, fearing I

would accidentally drop my towel at the same time I let out a snotty *achoo!* But Mom followed behind me. Apparently, I wasn't going to get out of this as easily as I'd wanted to. When my mom felt like she didn't know something, she usually latched on until she could work it out of me or figure it out herself. I decided to just dive right in. After all, she loved culture and the arts.

I squared my shoulders and prepared to tell the truth. "We just found out the school musical this year is *The Wiz* . . . and I was thinking about auditioning."

Mom's eyes widened. "Really?! You know I played Dorothy in a school version of the musical when I was little!"

"You did? I had no idea." Wow! My mom could sing and act? And she was a doctor now?! She was a star!

"Yeah, seventh or eighth grade. Had the dress and everything. This is great! Ah ha, you're following in your mom's footsteps."

"Well, I mean, I'm not much of a singer. At least not professionally," I added. I quickly threw on my pajamas.

"You don't need to be professional, honey. I'm just saying, if you want to audition, you should. I'd be proud of you either way! You clearly know the show. You know the words, the songs. Oh, your father will be so excited to hear this!"

I felt a chill go up my spine, and goose bumps formed

on my arms. "Noooooo!" I said, reaching out for mom's arm. She looked stunned at my reaction. But how could she not see it? Dad would never let me join the play. My dad, cofounder of his own law firm, was a serious guy. A book-smart, facts-and-figures kinda guy. He wanted me to pursue anything that would make my college applications as strong as possible. There's no way he'd support acting and singing in the school musical. He'd think it was a distraction from real academic work. What was I learning that could be applied to real skills? He'd never want me to spend any more time on the arts. Even getting him to agree to let me stay on the school paper staff was a struggle. How was I going to tell him I was officially choosing a school play over debate or future lawyer club or whatever else academic club he wanted to shove me into for my future? I *had* to keep him from finding out. It would only end in disaster. I started breathing faster just thinking about having to tell him.

I begged Mom in my sugary-sweetest voice: "Can we not tell him that I'm planning to audition? Or just not yet? I just want to tell him in my own way."

"Why not?" Mom asked, eyebrow crinkling with suspicion. She sat down on my bed.

How much of the truth could I tell here? I decided to reveal a bit of what I was thinking. "He might not think the school musical is 'serious enough.' Plus, I might not even

get a part! I definitely don't want to get him all worked up about something that might not even happen."

"Well, I think you have a great shot at making the cast," Mom said. "And I think no matter what, he'd be supportive. He's going to support any passion you have. When's the audition?"

"After Thanksgiving."

Mom grabbed my hand. "All right. Keep me posted on how you get on. Or if you need any help. Since, you know,

I have played the leading role before. I want my baby to nail her debut performance."

I smiled at my mom as she got up and left the room. If I got the role of Dorothy, I would be carrying on a family legacy, at least among the women, of starring in the role of Dorothy in *The Wiz.* My mom would be proud, and by default, her mother, my grandma, would be proud. And I would be proud, too! But that was the least of my worries. I knew there was absolutely no way I could tell my father I was even considering auditioning for the play. He would shut it down immediately, before I even gave myself a chance. No way, no how. This had to remain my secret . . . for now.

HONEST June

CONFESSION #28:

Victoria says I'm supposed to be living my truth at all times, in order for me to get this darn spell lifted. I've watched YouTube clips of *The Wiz* for hours since the principal made the announcement over the intercom this morning. And my mom says I have a great voice. But I know my dad won't support me.

He wouldn't like the idea of me spending more time on a "useless extracurricular" and less time on schoolwork. Less time studying will lead to bad grades. Bad grades lead to no colleges wanting me. No college means no career, no business cards with my name on them, no respect from the family. And then they'll disown me. Give me up for adoption. All because I wanted to act in one school musical. 😩

But I really do want to audition for the show. I know I've never acted before. But does that matter? There has to be a first time for everything.

How will I ever know if I could be a great actress if I don't try to be a great actress? Yes, Nia thinks the musical is lame. But she thinks everything is lame! I mean, she fell asleep during the dinosaur presentation during our fourth-grade field trip to the natural history museum, and that was AWESOME! At least Alvin thinks it's a cool idea to join the cast.

Do I risk embarrassing myself, going against the popular opinion of my friends, and disappointing my father to follow my heart and audition for the play? I have to be honest with myself. And if auditioning for the musical feels good in my spirit, then I should do it! Not because I want to become a professional actress, but at least to tell the truth, live my truth, and make some progress in getting this spell lifted.

CHAPTER SIX

"Do I haaaaaave to?" I asked Mom. On Wednesday she was still hounding me to tell Dad about the audition, even though it was two and a half weeks away. And I still didn't want to tell him until I was absolutely 100 percent sure I could even *get* a role in the play.

"Why don't you want to tell him?" Mom asked. "Sweetie, he'll be so proud!"

A weight started to fill my chest. Like a feeling of two heavy iron doors trying to protect my heart from attack, or protect my feelings from getting hurt. I just couldn't see Dad being super supportive of me wanting to pursue something so . . . *not* academic.

Every time one of our family friends or someone from

the neighborhood talks about how they are pursuing acting, or writing a book, or working on their music, Dad always calls it their "side hustle." As if none of those creative pursuits could possibly be considered real jobs. I mean, Featherstone Creek is just outside Atlanta, which is literally Black Hollywood. Tyler Perry owns a multi-gabillion-dollar studio here. Music producers are a dime a dozen here, and all of them have mansions and expensive cars and gold records lining their walls like subway tiles. So I knew it was possible to make a successful career out of the arts. . . . Plus, Dad just wasn't big into sharing thoughts and feelings to begin with—and isn't that what made someone

a good actor? A person who could draw on their inner thoughts and feelings and feed it into the character they were playing? Sounded like Dad's worst nightmare.

"Honey, there's more than one way to be successful besides going to school and being a doctor, lawyer, or accountant, you know," I overheard Mom say to Dad once.

"Of course I know," Dad had replied. "But the more time spent studying books to earn a degree, the more likely the success."

"You can get a degree in film production these days, dear," Mom had said to him. "Steven Spielberg has one. Look at him."

"Yeah, but he's Spielberg. Besides, he dropped out to make a movie!"

"Spike Lee?"

"I'm just saying, Audrey. Actors, musicians . . . it's hard to be the next Halle Berry or Quincy Jones. If you wanted to be an actress, your multigenerational MD family in Featherstone Creek would have provided for you if you didn't make it. But you're not most people. Not everyone has family to fall back on," he had said pointedly.

Dad had sat me down a few weeks ago to tell me how hard it had been for him to work his way up to being a lawyer. He didn't have a successful, wealthy family to support him like my mom did—he had to do it all himself. And even though he and Mom were successful, I could only imagine how much he would talk me out of following the unknown path of the arts on principle.

My thoughts pulled me back to the present. "You know he hates theater," I blurted out to my mom. I didn't know if that was entirely true. *Oh, now watch, Victoria's going to find me!* "Well, it *seems* like it anyway . . . ," I said, correcting myself. *Phew, that's better.* "I didn't think he was a big fan of, like, creative types. He always cracks jokes that actors need to get real jobs to get health insurance."

"No, he doesn't," Mom replied. "And you think Michael B. Jordan needs a side hustle to get health insurance? He plays superheroes in huge-budget Hollywood movies!"

"Okay, that's one example," I said. "But Dad's not really going to be cool with his daughter pursuing those things. You know, Mr. Howard Law. You saw what happened when I didn't want to do debate team."

"That was different," Mom said. "For one, you insulted him when you told him you didn't want to do it. And for two, he's already told you he'd support any new endeavor you were really passionate about."

"Yeah, but that's another thing! I don't even know if I'll get a role. That's why I was going to wait until I auditioned. If I don't get a part, then why bother him with the news? But if I do, then that proves I'm actually good at acting, and then he'll be more likely to be nice about it."

Mom stood in front of me for a few seconds, silent,

then cupped her hand around my chin. "You'll get a role if you want this bad enough. You'll rehearse, and you'll sing your heart out, and you'll achieve whatever you want to achieve. And your dad will support you no matter what. I'll make sure of it."

✦

For the past week, I'd been rehearsing any spare moment I could, particularly when Dad wasn't home. He had been working late on a few cases, which bought me some extra time in the evenings. But my best time to rehearse was in the morning on my walk to school, humming the songs to myself while Nia and Olive gossiped about friends and what they saw on Instagram, or waiting for Mom to pick me up after class. Like today, a Friday afternoon, Mom was late picking me up from school because she had an unexpected delivery, so I watched more YouTube clips of Diana Ross singing in the movie while I was waiting.

When Mom pulled up, she saw the video playing on

my phone in my hand. "Ah, practicing any moment you can get?"

"Yup," I said.

"You tell your dad yet?" Mom asked, knowing full well I had not.

I looked at her with pleading eyes. I really didn't want to disrupt dinner tonight, much less my concentration ahead of the audition in a few weeks, with this kind of pressure. It was bound to turn into a big argument, and I couldn't handle that before seeing if I even had the chops to make the cast.

Mom took pity on me. "Okay, you can hold off on telling your father until you see if you make the cast. Audition. Then tell him as soon as you find out if you've made it. Time's ticking, kiddo."

✦

I retreated to my room after dinner that night so I could avoid any questions from Dad. I thought about what he might say if I told him I was auditioning. I could hear him now: "Don't think about becoming an actress before graduating college."

Just thinking about his reaction made me feel short of breath, and I had a headache coming on. Then I spotted

dust floating in front of my eyes. A funnel cloud formed in front of me, spinning rapidly. I knew who was about to drop in for another visit. Victoria. The last person I wanted to see.

A female form popped out in front of me, the tiara on her head cocked over to one side. "June, my darling! How are you?"

I coughed, clearing my throat of the fairy dust her funnel cloud of magic had kicked up around the room. "Victoria."

I thought about how Victoria tended to follow me around during the day. Did she literally walk behind me from class to class, invisible to everyone else, just like a ghost? Was she sitting at the cafeteria table alongside us when we were all talking about the play? Or did she shape-shift, transforming into, say, the body of Mrs. Worth, so she could see us through the eyes of real people? Or did she remain floating fairy dust until I attempted to lie, sparking the dust to take form and produce Victoria? I was still unclear on how she appeared right at the most annoying times, but the woman *seriously* had a knack for it.

She straightened her tiara. "This thing is so heavy . . . ah, better. So, let's deal with the task at hand! *Love* that you're going to audition for the school musical, June, darling! But when exactly are you planning to tell your father about it?"

I groaned. I knew I was supposed to tell the truth. Victoria wasn't going to like it, but I had to be honest about . . . not being honest.

"I'm not planning to tell him now. Or anytime soon."

"Why not, June?"

"I just told him I didn't want to go to law school like a minute ago! Why disappoint him again so soon?"

"Who says he'll be disappointed? He wants you to pursue whatever makes you happy."

Victoria waved her magic wand in front of my face, and then over my head and shoulders. "How do you feel when you think about the school musical? When you sing the songs to yourself, or in the shower like you did the day the principal made the announcement?"

I thought about the time I'd spent rehearsing the songs and dances this past week ahead of my audition. How the movements felt natural. How the singing seemed to help me calm down, even when my stomach was fluttering with nervousness about stuff I was usually freaked out about, like school and all my responsibilities and commitments and potentially upsetting my parents or friends. Focusing on *The Wiz* made me feel . . . it made me feel . . .

"I feel really happy."

"Yeah, I can tell. Just the mere mention of *The Wiz* makes you smile."

I guessed I was smiling in front of her pretty big. Victoria turned me to face my mirror and leaned toward me. "June, you should tell your dad as soon as possible. Your mom has been supportive, and I'm sure he will be, too. If he needs a good reason as to why you're doing it, your smile will be enough. Tell him the truth. Don't forget, the only way you'll get the spell lifted is if you tell the truth at all times—to everyone, even if you're worried about how they'll react."

Victoria stepped back a few paces from me and began to turn around. She kicked up fairy dust once again, turning faster and faster until a tight tornado of glitter covered her body. Then, in a poof, she disappeared into thin air, leaving me alone with my thoughts.

Maybe Dad *would* be happy for me. I mean, he did promise to support things that made me happy after we had our big talk about me not knowing if being a lawyer was what I wanted to do. And besides, I was only eleven! I had no idea what I wanted to be when I grew up. All I knew was now, in sixth grade, in my first year at Featherstone Creek Middle School, I wanted to be a part of the school musical because *The Wiz* was the most magical show I'd ever seen.

I heard a buzzing sound coming from my book bag, and I realized I was getting a video call. I reached for my phone. *Chloe!*

"Hey, girl!" she said. "What's cracking?"

"Nothing, just over here plotting my new career path as an actrizzzzz."

"Whaaat? Since when?"

"Since they announced they are putting on a production of *The Wiz* at school."

"Cool! You've seen that movie like a thousand times. You'd be a great Dorothy!"

"You think?" I asked. I let myself visualize landing the lead. Wearing those sparkly silver shoes. Dancing arm in arm with the Scarecrow, Lion, and Tinman. Clicking my heels three times to get myself back home while holding on to my dear puppy, Toto.

"But I've never acted before," I said, my doubt bubbling back up to the surface. It was one thing to audition for the show and end up a Munchkin or a Winkie—but it was quite another to think I had a shot at getting the lead role.

"But you know how to study and memorize schoolwork, like formulas and facts and stuff. Same thing. Memorizing lines. Reciting them back. You got this."

It *was* the same thing. Roughly. I visualized myself on the stage, singing and dancing. If I got a background role in the chorus, at least I could just dance my way out of forgetting any lyrics.

"Let's rehearse right now! Let me hear it—'Can you! Feel a! Brand new day!'" Chloe said, breaking out into song. I couldn't help but sing and dance along. I propped the phone up on some books on my desk and began dancing around my room. Chloe clapped and followed along, dancing around her room, too. I got caught up in the rhythm, the rush of the song, just like Diana Ross did

when she sang along with a hundred Winkies that transform from ugly to beautiful, free dancers. Free, happy, light, and optimistic.

That was me.

"You're right," I told Chloe, realization dawning upon me. "I'm going to audition for the role of Dorothy!"

CHAPTER SEVEN

I was on the field, running as fast as I could. Blake had already scored a goal, Kenya Barrett had scored the other, and we'd kept the other team to just one goal for the whole match. I had been in good position to score twice, chucking the ball toward the opponents' goal with power and only missing it by inches. But then, on the last minute of the fourth quarter, Blake passed me the ball, and I hauled it toward the end of the field. I hurled the ball toward the net with a twist of the wrist, and *whap!* It hit the back of the opponents' net. We'd won! Game, set, and the end of field hockey season had arrived.

I could hear my dad cheering from the stands on the opposite end of the field. "All right! That's my baby!" he

cried out. Blake and Kenya and the rest of the team high-fived and whooped and hollered. This was an amazing moment. We'd won! On a goal I'd scored! I was stoked! And I loved having people cheer my name.

But in the back of my mind, my self-doubt crept back up again. I thought about me onstage, starring in *The Wiz*. I thought about getting these sorts of cheers and applause for a musical I was singing and dancing in. One where I was putting my heart on display. I wondered, would my dad be just as proud? Would he cheer just as loudly? Would my friends support me just as much? My heart started beating faster as my mind raced down the rabbit hole.

As we drove home, my dad went on and on about the match. "You looked good out there, June! Quick, responsive. Look how far you've come in one season. You'll be an all-star next year!"

"Thanks," I said. My teeth clenched. I wrung my hands together out of nervousness in the back seat. I thought about what his face might look like if I told him I wanted to start performing onstage. Field hockey season was over, Thanksgiving was a few days away—I should've been feeling light and free and happy, but instead I was filled with anxiety.

✦

Thanksgiving at my house was busy. Even though Mom was mostly out delivering babies and seeing patients, she always made the holiday dinner. Monday night the turkey was already thawing in the refrigerator. Tuesday meant that the time to organize cookware and table settings had come. Wednesday night, we baked the desserts. Thursday's cooking started at dawn. Grandma, my mom's mom, usually came over then, and the two of them would cook all day, including a big breakfast for us in between.

"Help me with these brussels sprouts while you eat

your breakfast," Mom said as I came downstairs in my pajamas.

"Brussels sprouts?" I said. "Since when did we start making brussels sprouts on Thanksgiving?"

Grandma and Mom looked at each other, then looked at me. "Since I said so," Mom said, eyebrow raised.

I could think of no fewer than thirty vegetables I would eat before I voluntarily ate brussels sprouts. The smell alone made me wrinkle up my face. And they are hard as rocks when they are raw! I looked at the bag. I felt a tickle in my nose. The truth was literally itching to come out of me.

"What?" my mom said.

"Brussels sprouts," I said, clenching my teeth. "Not my fave."

"You liked them when we went to the Crab Shack?"

I clenched my teeth even harder and started rubbing my nose. I felt an urge to sneeze coming on. I did eat the ones at the Crab Shack restaurant, because they were covered in maple syrup and crunchy onions. But Mom was going to sauté these, then season them lightly with olive oil and pepper and make them all healthy. They were going to taste like hard air.

But I couldn't tell her that. I could literally feel Victoria's fairy godmother breath on my shoulder. I told her my real feelings in a softer way.

"Maybe the way you make them isn't my fave," I said.

Mom looked at me. Oh, man, I knew she was mad now. See what the truth did? I'd done this before: told people what I really thought so I could prove to Victoria I was living my truth or whatever she wanted me to do, and yet, people still got mad, and the spell still hovered over me! This is why I wrote my real opinions in my secret blog, so I didn't get that look from people. Ugh, now I'd just ruined Thanksgiving dinner.

"You know what, I got these. You go on now." My mom turned back to chopping up some onions, losing herself in the task of cooking to forget about my opinions of her cooking.

Greeeeaaaaaaaattt! I thought. Probably not a good time to ask if she made my favorite sweet potato pie now. Dang it, Victoria!

✦

Lee and his grandparents were always invited to our Thanksgiving feast, especially since Lee's parents were still at sea in the service.

Lee and I hadn't talked much since he'd asked about Nia. And to be honest, I'd been avoiding him at school. But I was looking forward to spending some downtime with him. Spending Thanksgiving together was tradition, and I was glad to have the chance to see him.

While the adults and anyone over five feet tall cooked food, and the football game blared on the television in the background, Lee suddenly looked over at me with a sly grin on his face. "Let's bike to my house and check on Chadwick. You've never met him."

This was big. *Huge.*

He'd had Chadwick for a few months already, but no one had met him except for Lee's best pal, Alvin. Lee's pet was the most important creature in his life. He was like Lee's beloved son. And Lee had basically just invited me to meet him. This was a big deal. This meant something. Right?

We rode our bikes over to his house, a few minutes' ride from mine. The crisp fall air was cool enough to need a sweater, but the sunshine kept it from getting too chilly out. We arrived at his place and dumped our bikes in the driveway, then opened the fence to the backyard.

Lee ushered us onto the patio. "He's this way. He's in a good mood today."

Lee opened the back door that led into the kitchen and living room. A large tank sat on a table near the back of the room. I stepped up to peer inside, and there was Chadwick. The lizard looked at me with wide eyes, sticking his tongue out at me every few seconds. He was bigger than a mouse, but smaller than a hamster. When Lee stuck his hand into the glass cage, Chadwick calmly stepped into his open palm.

Lee reached out to me. "You can hold him," he said. "Here."

I figured the moment would have to come at some point, but I was *not* enthusiastic about the idea of holding a slimy lizard. I wasn't into cold-blooded creatures because they aren't furry and cuddly. If I could just hold in my words of disgust, maybe Victoria wouldn't send a lying signal my way? I couldn't tell Lee how I felt, obviously. And I was also super nervous I might freak out and drop him if I thought about it more. And then Lee would never trust me with his pets, or anything else, again.

So I held out my sweaty hand, and Lee plopped the lizard right on. I felt my knees grow woozy, but I held on, feeling each of Chadwick's prickly feet step onto my skin. I clenched my teeth as he settled into my palm. And then, he sat there. "Do you like him?" Lee asked.

I kept clenching my teeth. I much preferred to hold something like a hamster or gerbil. But this was Lee's pet. His pride and joy. And he was happy I was holding him. I kept smiling, even though I wasn't happy. *Am I lying by smiling right now?!*

"He likes you," Lee said. He looked at me, elated, as if his project at the school science fair had successfully deployed.

I looked at Chadwick. He was cute, for a lizard, admittedly. I'd never seen a reptile so, like, chill before. And the longer he stayed in my hand, the more relaxed I got. "Wow, I've never seen him so comfortable in someone else's hand besides mine before," Lee said. He was beaming like a proud parent.

We both stood there staring at this innocent creature, Lee's shoulder touching mine. I felt that weird tingly sensation again, the one that felt like I had just chugged sparkling water. My heart felt like it had an extra beat to its rhythm. I didn't have this feeling when I stood next to anyone else.

"I'll put his food in the dish, and then we can bounce,"

Lee said. He reached for some of Chadwick's lizard food, which to me looked like mushy sawdust, and scooped a cupful out and put it in the feeding dish in the tank. Then Lee grabbed Chadwick from my hand and placed him back into the tank. Chadwick chowed down, clearly hungry, and Lee replaced the top on the tank.

"He's set. Now we eat," Lee said, and grinned. "Let's go."

✦

Back at my house, we sat down for a mostly delicious meal for Thanksgiving. The turkey, which my dad had cooked, was on point. As was the gravy. And the yams, even if Mom didn't put the marshmallows on top like all the families in those TV ads do. "Too much sugar, honey," she'd said when I asked if she would.

"It's yams; it's supposed to have sugar!" I had protested. "What, you going to take the brown sugar out of the pecan pie next?"

"Watch yourself, June," Mom had said. This was now the second time me telling her how I really felt about her Thanksgiving menu had earned me a sharp-tongued response.

Meanwhile, the stuffing was next level. I mean, can anyone really mess up stuffing? I guess if you added too much water, maybe, turning it into a paste? It's still really hard to mess up.

I thought it was impossible to mess up corn bread, too, until I took a bite of the one Lee's grandmother had made. It was blackened on the edges. And heavy and dense, like a brick. I took a bite and almost broke a tooth off.

"You like it, baby?" Lee's grandmother turned to me.

I froze. I couldn't lie to the old lady. To *Lee's* old lady. But I could not get my teeth through this hard corn-and-butter baked good. I kept my mouth closed around the yellow substance. My eyes darted from Lee's grandmother, to Lee, to my mother, to Lee's grandmother.

"I think that's a yes?" Lee said.

I nodded. Lee had saved me! Grandma smiled and looked back down at her plate. But I felt the itch in my nose building up. In a few seconds it was like the burnt corn crumbs from the corn bread had shot up my nose. I had to sneeze. I had to inhale. I had to exhale. Which meant I had to shoot the corn bread out of my mouth and across the table in front of Lee and his grandmother and my father and the rest of our dinner guests.

Aaachhooo!—Phlleewum!—Plop! The hunk of chewed-up corn bread bounced across the table and landed in front of my dad.

Everyone looked at me. I had nowhere to run, nowhere to turn. Nothing to do but tell the truth.

"The corn bread kicked up my allergies!" I blurted.

I had graduated from the kiddie table to the adult table just a few years ago. Now, by launching my corn bread across the table, I knew I had disinvited myself from every family feast for the next millennium.

"June!" my mother exclaimed.

"I'm sorry!" I said, and got up quickly, too horrified from embarrassment to sit in front of my elders any longer. I ran into my bedroom and tried to scoot myself underneath my bed to hide for the rest of the night. But my mother found me, ushered me back to the dining table, and made me apologize to everyone on the spot. "I'm sorry I spat my corn bread out," I said in an embarrassed tone.

"You should get yourself an antihistamine for those allergies, June," Lee's grandmother said.

What I needed was an anti-Victoria-mine for my issues. I'll take two, please.

✦

The day after Thanksgiving, Nia and Olive came over to my house. We wanted to scour the Black Friday sales online. Mom was home from the hospital making some turkey soup from the leftovers we had from Thanksgiving dinner, and Dad was getting some work done at the office, so I knew any mentions of the school musical wouldn't reach his ears. I could rest easy for just a bit.

Nia and Olive arrived together, having ridden their bikes from Nia's house.

"Heyyyyyy," I said to my pals. Nia's braids were tucked under a New York Yankees cap, and Olive's curls were freshly fluffed from the crisp fall air blowing through her hair as she biked.

"Hey, girl," Nia said as she strode into my house and took her hat off. Her long braids swayed across her back as she walked by me into the kitchen. "Snacks first, then shopping."

We went to the refrigerator and grabbed a bowl of grapes, then took some popcorn and a bag of pecans and dried cranberries from the pantry and headed upstairs.

Nia breezed into my bedroom. Olive pulled out her tablet and Nia was already on her phone, looking through social media for coupons and discount codes.

"So, y'all," Nia started. "What about Lee?"

"What about Lee?" I asked. But I knew exactly what about Lee she wanted to know. *Oh man, here we go.* The moment I'd been dreading.

"You know, *what about Lee?*"

Olive turned her head to one side. "What about Lee, as in what do we think of him? As in, do we think he's . . . you know . . ."

"Yeah, Olive, that," Nia confirmed.

"*Why* are we asking?" I spat back. Again, another question I already knew the answer to.

"Because, you know, I think he's, like, cute and stuff."

A fire grew in my belly. Nia of all people knew that I had . . . feelings for Lee. Though I hadn't been good at expressing exactly what those feelings were. But now it was clear to me that Nia had some kind of feelings for him, too. Maybe even . . . *a crush*.

But I do feel some type of way, even if I don't know *what* type of way. If I like Lee, can Nia like him, too? Is that allowed? It sounded . . . greedy!

"Why all of a sudden do you like him?" I blurted out.

"Because he's cool," Nia said.

Cool?! Lee wore his dad's old flannel shirts to school! It wasn't the first word I'd use to describe him!

Nia continued, "And nice. I needed help in math class the other day and he gave me his notes. And didn't poke fun at me or anything."

What was going on? Did I see hearts and birds chirping around Nia's head as she talked to us about Lee? My Lee? Creek-loving Lee? The one with the pet lizard? I don't understand.

"Anyway, I'm just saying . . . you think he might like me?"

"No!" I blurted out. I felt an itch in my nose. I needed to come clean quick or else I'd have a Victoria-induced sneezing fit. I felt the sneeze coming. . . . Oh my bleezus, "I mean . . . I don't mean that!"

It was too late. *"Achoo-achoo-achooo!"*

"Bless you!" Olive said. "You got allergies?"

"No!" I said, flustered. I looked for a Kleenex or a scarf or something. I could feel my eyes getting itchy. Another sneeze attack was coming. "I mean—*ahh-ahhh-aacckkchoo!*"

"What I mean is—*achoo-achoo!*" *Geez, STOP SNEEZING!* "He's very nice, yes."

That was a truth. And my nose stopped itching for two seconds. Nia and Olive looked at me, puzzled. "You okay?" Nia asked.

"Yes! I'm fine!" I said. I walked into my closet pretending to look for something, but I really just wanted to hide my face from Nia. I knew I should have told her about Lee. I knew it was my duty as her best friend to let her know her crush had the same feelings for her as she did for him. And Lee had asked me specifically to invite Nia to hang out with us. I had to do it. This was my opportunity.

But I couldn't.

I wasn't exactly lying by saying nothing. If I stayed hiding in my closet, I could avoid the conversation. Then I wouldn't have to reveal anything. That technically wasn't lying, right?

"Girl, you okay in there?" Nia asked.

"Fine!" I said. "I figured out what I need to do first—clean this closet. I have so many old clothes in here!"

"Um, okay," Nia said. "Whatever you think."

Suddenly, Mom called us from downstairs. "Girls, you want some lunch? I've got some soup ready."

Leftovers could not have come at a better time. I could have buried myself under all my dirty clothes in that closet just to avoid telling Nia the truth about Lee. But now that we'd been called to lunch we could eat, laugh, and forget all about Lee and Nia's quest to get to know each other better.

✦

I made it through the rest of our hangout without speaking about Lee by keeping my mouth filled with something—turkey soup, a spoon, a handful of popcorn, leftover sweet potato pie—at all times. The only words I could really get out were "Umm hrmphf," "Mmm-nnnmm," and "Umm-mmm." But really that's all I needed to communicate that the soup was delicious, Nia shouldn't buy that purple hair crimper just because it was on sale because she'd never use it, and I really needed the bath bomb set for my mom because she could use a fun self-care-themed stocking stuffer.

After a good amount of Thanksgiving leftovers and buying one hair straightener, three nail art kits, and the glitter bath bomb set, Nia and Olive headed out. I retreated back to my room, exhausted from having to hold back the truth about Lee. I know I should have just blurted out at some point that Lee wanted to hang out with Nia. But my throat tightened up every time I tried. Or was it my heart tightening up? It was hard to tell exactly what was keeping me from revealing the truth. It was time to turn to my blog. I'd realized in the past few weeks I'd begun to write in my blog multiple times a day—about the small stuff and the big stuff. It felt like the one place I could turn without being judged, or hurting someone's feelings with the truth. I dove right in.

HONEST June

CONFESSION #50:

Why oh why oh why is this happening? Lee and Nia! They both have feelings for each other, and I'm the only one that knows and I should be telling both of them how the other feels and I just can't. Why does Lee like Nia? Nia's pretty. I get it. But she's materialistic. And petty. And she hates lizards! Is Lee really going to pick Nia over his pet lizard? Chadwick will be crushed.

And Nia knows that I like him. Well, do I like him? I think I like him . . . ? I mean, I've never admitted to her that I do like him, whenever she's asked. But since she's asking, she must know I like him. She knows and she's still going after him. That's pretty low! I feel betrayed. 🥺

Suddenly the air shifted in my room. I felt a chill and reached for a sweatshirt hanging off the back of my desk chair. Then I sneezed, even though I hadn't lied. Maybe that was straight-up allergies? Or . . . nope . . . I knew what that was. Ugh, why does Victoria always show up when I'm not in the mood to talk?!

A storm cloud of glitter and fairy dust swirled in the middle of my room, which gave way to a recognizable female form. My fairy godmother had arrived, ready to deliver a lesson or a lecture or some other annoyance. The dust cloud blew my papers off my desk and ruffled my bedding.

"Well, hello there, June. Long time no see!" Victoria said excitedly.

"Not long enough," I mumbled.

"Oh, June, as I've reminded you time and time again, I am here to help you improve your life, not make it worse!"

"Ha!" I laughed loudly. "I have crazy receipts to show how you and your fairy dust and your silly spell have gotten me in super-awkward situations!"

"Anyway," Victoria said, "we have lots to catch up on. I saw that whole interaction between you and Nia about Lee. Why didn't you tell your best friend that your other best friend has equal feelings for her, too?"

I rocked back in my desk chair. "Because maybe I didn't

want to get in the middle of it," I said defensively. "That's between them. I shouldn't have to play Cupid."

Victoria scrunched up her face. "It's not about playing Cupid. The big thing is you didn't tell Nia the truth. Nia asked you what you thought of Lee and you said nothing. Living your truth under the spell is not just about not lying. You must reveal the truth when asked. You can't stay silent and avoid telling people your real feelings."

I didn't know what to say. First, I didn't know how to explain what type of feelings I was having for Lee. And I certainly didn't want to admit that I had any kind of feelings to *anyone*, especially Nia. I truly didn't know what to say to either of them, and I had no idea how to explain any of this to Victoria.

"Do you want to have the spell lifted?" Victoria said after a moment of silence.

"It would be my dream come true," I said, putting my palms together in front of my heart.

"Then you have to put in the work. You must express the truth whenever the opportunity's presented to you. That means you're gonna have to tell Nia that Lee wants to hang out with her the next chance you get."

I pouted. If I was going to tell the truth, the whole truth, and nothing but, there was no way I could avoid telling Nia that I also had some kind of feelings for Lee—and had for a long time.

"But won't it hurt her even more to know we both potentially like the same boy? And that the boy would have to choose between the two of us! Besides, Lee and I have been friends the longest and we both like the outdoors and lakes and stuff and I've met his pet lizard! What does Nia have in common with him? There's no way he'd choose her over me!" I exclaimed.

"Or . . ." Victoria raised a finger to her chin, mulling another possibility. "Maybe Lee doesn't like you the same way he likes Nia, June. And you're scared to admit that."

I looked away from Victoria. My hands started to get sweaty, and my mouth felt like it was full of cotton balls. My lower lip trembled. What if Lee did like Nia more than me?

"Either way," Victoria said, "I'm going to remind you again what you need to do: no lying, and no hiding. I need to see you are openly telling the truth about everything—no matter if it's something you don't agree with—to everyone in your life. That's the only way I will drop the spell. The more truth you tell, the closer you get to being free of me. Once you prove that you have found a way tell the truth no matter what, the spell will be lifted. Those are the stakes. Got it?"

I nodded softly. I wondered if it were possible to self-isolate in my room as if I were on punishment without actually being on punishment. That way I wouldn't have to see anyone and risk revealing anything at all.

"Cheer up," Victoria said—she must've seen the dejected look on my face. "I think this is going to be an opportunity to bring two of your closest friends closer. More love to go around!"

I wasn't so sure I wanted that.

Victoria stood in front of my bed and flicked her magic wand a few times. A cloud of sparkles and dust surrounded her, then carried her up into thin air, leaving a small trail of dust behind as a reminder to me that she was always watching.

CONFESSION #51:

I just can't believe it. I mean, Nia and Lee potentially dating goes against everything that I had planned for my future—Lee and I being best of friends, telling each other everything, even things we didn't tell people like Alvin and Nia, and then going to college together and finally after all these years—in school together, taking the same classes, and going on family vacations—him confessing his feelings for me on graduation day, getting engaged after one of us finishes medical school (likely him, but could be me), and moving back to Featherstone Creek to become the mayor and first lady. 👫

Okay, this is one of the many fantasies I had about our future that I dared. Not. Tell. Anyone. Especially Nia. And I don't plan on telling anyone any of this for a very long time. But Victoria won't release me from this spell unless I confess. How am I going to get around this? I can't even describe what I'm feeling, much less tell two people who may actually want the same thing I do. This is hard. Super hard. Maybe I can avoid them both so I don't have to tell either one of them anything. I need to distract myself with schoolwork and the musical. Maybe if I focus on those things my brain won't have any space to deal with the pressure of telling Nia and Lee the truth.

CHAPTER EIGHT

It was the first day of school after Thanksgiving break. I woke up with a strange feeling in my stomach, like there were some undigested Pop Rocks firing around in there. Even though I stayed up late to watch more YouTube videos of *The Wiz* clips, my eyes woke up before my alarm went off. I sprang upright in bed. A smile grew across my face. Audition day had arrived.

I turned on the shower and, with sounds of the water hiding my singing, I went into a version of "Brand New Day" to practice and to hype me up. The auditions were after school, and we needed to sing a song from whatever section of the show we preferred. I felt like "Home" would be the song that would help me best nail the part of Dorothy.

I hummed to myself as I went down to breakfast; my father packed up his briefcase for work as I came down. "Morning, June," he said while deep in thought about his own day. He gave me a kiss on the forehead and dashed off. "Have a good day at school," he said, totally unaware that today could be one of the most awesome—or humiliating—days of my life.

I ate two bowls of cereal. I don't remember tasting either one. I looked over more YouTube clips. And then I got ready to walk with Nia and Olive to school like normal.

The girls waved at me from the end of the driveway, just like usual.

"You ready for your big audition?" Olive asked.

"I think so," I said, as true an answer as I could express. But I was so anxious about the audition, I didn't say anything else as we walked to school. My brain was laser-focused on every word of "Home." I sang it under my breath as we walked, analyzing how I hit each note, how I pronounced each word. I wanted to be as perfect as could be. As perfect as I could be with sweaty palms and butterflies in the tummy from nerves.

I took deep breaths as we walked into the school. I almost ran into Mrs. Worth on the way to my locker before my lunch period because my nose was buried in my tablet playing clips from the musical. The school day went by in a blur—I hardly paid attention to what was happening around me, I was so caught up in my head about the audition. And then, finally, the end of the day arrived, and I walked into the school auditorium, ready to audition.

Nervous energy bubbled in my tummy once again. I walked toward the stage, past the English teacher for each grade, the dance teacher, and the drama teacher, Mrs. Stevens, who were all seated at a long table toward the front with clipboards in front of them.

Mrs. Stevens greeted me. "Hello there."

"Hi," I said quietly from the stage, and cleared my throat. I needed to remember to project from the stage, right?

"Your name for the group, please?"

"June. June Jackson."

"Great, June. What are you going to perform for us?"

"I'm going to sing 'Home,'" I said. None of the judges looked impressed. They gazed down at their pads with their pens in their hands and nodded. I stood there at the front of the stage, not wanting to make a noise before they did.

"You can begin, June."

I started singing. As soon as the notes floated away from my mouth, it felt like the butterflies and the tension in my stomach disappeared. I belted out the words with force, power, even. I had not one worry or thought on my mind as I sang. I couldn't even feel my feet standing on the stage. Maybe I had floated up at some point?

I closed my eyes and hit the last note, letting the vibration of the note rattle my vocal cords. I leaned back for emphasis, my arms outstretched, then I closed my mouth, stood upright, and finally opened my eyes again. The judges looked directly at me with wide eyes. Then they clapped.

"Well done, June," said Mrs. Stevens. "Thanks for coming out."

I didn't know if I was Dorothy material. But I felt good afterward. I walked down the stairs to the left of the stage feeling confident. Smiling.

"Woooooow!" I heard a voice from the back of the auditorium. Alvin stood up and clapped his hands as I walked toward the exit doors.

"You were listening the whole time?"

"Not the whole time, just while I wait for my turn. I had no idea you could sing like that."

"I usually just sing in the shower. But I have been obsessed with this musical since I was, like, super young."

"Well, you probably just got yourself the lead role," Alvin said.

I blushed and blinked fast. "Noooooo, there're more girls auditioning and stuff. Even seventh and eighth graders!"

"Don't sell yourself short, June," Alvin said, then walked up the aisle to the stage for his audition.

I smiled as I turned away from the doors and gathered my things to head out.

✦

After the audition, I waited for Nia and Olive to finish up with their extracurriculars so we could walk home together.

"How'd it go?" Olive asked first. Nia was on her phone texting, as if she had more pressing news to catch up on.

"I think it went okay," I said. "Alvin thinks I did really well. But who knows? Hard to read the reaction from Mrs. Stevens and the other teachers."

"Right," said Olive. "I'm sure you'll get a role, if not *the* role."

Nia kept looking at her phone. It was as if she'd rather get braces than encourage me after my audition. "You see Ayanna Pullman is in LA right now?" she finally said. "Guess she didn't audition. Maybe you do have a shot, June."

My heart wanted to be annoyed with Nia, but hearing that Ayanna was gone was slightly encouraging. If there was one less person to compete for the role of Dorothy, maybe I did have a chance to get the part!

The three of us walked home, holding our coats close around our necks as a chilly breeze blew through the leaves. I walked a few steps ahead of the girls, anxious energy still charging through my veins. My mind replayed my performance over and over, analyzing my singing. Did I remember all the words to the song? Did I enunciate enough during the second verse? Could I have been more

animated in my performance? My train of thought was only broken by Nia's voice going, "June! Your house. You going home tonight?"

I looked to the right. My house was just in front of us. "Um, yeah, see you guys later," I said.

"Keep us posted on the auditions," Olive said with a smile. As if there was anything else I'd be thinking about!

HONEST June

CONFESSION #62:

I did it. I auditioned! I gave it my all and I feel okay! In fact, for something that seemed so new and scary, I actually felt at ease onstage. Even Alvin thought I did a pretty great job. And that means a lot coming from him, considering he, like, sings in front of people all the time. (He's really nice. . . . I think he'd make a really great Scarecrow.) But, of course, Nia had to throw shade. "Ayanna Pullman's out of town, so you might have a shot!"

All those anxiety feelings that I have before a big test or when I'm nervous about my dad's reaction about something or when I'm around Lee lately didn't happen when I sang onstage for the first time in front of my teachers. No headaches, no stomach pains. I felt . . . super chill? I'm still smiling! Maybe theater could be the best thing to happen to me?

CHAPTER NINE

I did what I could to distract myself from thinking about the audition the next few days as we waited for the cast list to be posted. I studied every single note I'd taken throughout the day for each class. I was completely caught up on my homework for the first time all year. I cleaned the kitchen after dinner and took out the trash. I studied even more (then I cleaned my room, too). I called Chloe but forbade her to talk about the audition—I didn't want to jinx it. ("Girl, then why are we even on the phone?" she asked. "Because I don't want to hear my own thoughts!" I explained.)

I had that crazy roller-coaster feeling in my stomach for three days. Not crazy like I wanted to throw up, not queasy like anxiety. Not like I was going to have another panic attack because I was freaking out. More like anticipation. Like when you're excited to go on a trip somewhere.

When I sat in class, I couldn't get comfortable in my chair. It's like I was tensing my body to control butterflies floating around in my stomach. I tried to distract myself by doodling in my notebook and deep breathing and taking extra-thorough notes of every little thing our teachers said—even noting when other kids asked questions—but it was no use. My mind was preoccupied with *The Wiz*. I literally couldn't wait to see the cast list!

After school, I tried to concentrate on my homework, but my head hurt thinking about whether I'd sung well enough to impress the teachers making decisions about the cast. I had wrung my mind in a knot.

Then I thought about what would happen if I made the play but didn't get cast as Dorothy. What if I was cast as a Winkie? Would my dad even come to the play if I was just a Winkie? At least if I was Dorothy, I would be in the lead role. He'd have to be proud of me if I starred in the lead role! But if I was a Winkie, he'd think I didn't have enough acting chops to get a starring role, and therefore wouldn't be an exceptional, Halle Berry–level actress and therefore wouldn't be able to make it as an actress or afford healthcare or my own apartment, and he'd tell me to get a real job. Thus killing my dreams of being an actress, a creative, an artist. My whole life would be spent behind some desk somewhere, wondering *what if* . . .

So his support all hinged on me scoring the role of Dorothy.

That was a lot of pressure for my first try at acting.

✦

Finally, Tuesday morning had arrived. The day when the cast would be announced.

Mrs. Stevens was supposed to post the lineup for the theater production on the wall of the auditorium before school started. I was waiting for Nia and Olive outside for twenty minutes before they made it to the end of my driveway. "Okay, let's go!" I said, springing ahead of them. "Come on, guys, come on come on come on come on come on. . . ."

"What's the rush?" Nia said.

"They're announcing the cast for the play!" I said. "And I want to see if I made the cut."

"Oh, right, right, let's hustle!" Olive said. "What if you get the lead? Oh, June, that would be major!"

"Yeah, it would," Nia said. "Major for a school play. This is a school production, after all, not Broadway. It's gonna be okay."

I looked at Nia. My temples were already throbbing

from thinking about whether I would get a part in this play. Now my jaw was hurting from clenching my teeth as Nia yet again acted like she didn't care about my dreams. "This is probably one of the biggest things I've done since I started middle school. So, yeah, it's major."

"Okay, girl, dang," Nia said. "I didn't know you took it so seriously."

"I do," I said, daggers shooting out of my eyes at her. "So I want you to take it seriously."

Nia blinked quickly, looking for something to say. "Sorry, I'm just not into theater."

"But you're into celebrities, right?" I said. "So imagine me walking the red carpet at the Oscars in like fifteen years with you as my plus-one. Sound fun? Well, it all starts with this musical."

"All right, all right, June," Nia said, "or should I say, Dorothy."

"Thank you," I replied. I could still hear the hint of shade in her voice. But I'd said my piece. No time for haters right now.

I kept two paces ahead of them the entire time we walked to school. Once we got onto school property, I sped ahead of the girls and headed for the auditorium. "I'll keep you posted," I said over my shoulder.

"Good luck!" Olive called out.

I nervously made my way to the theater wing, walking

quickly, that excited feeling popping into my stomach again. My palms were sweaty. I tried to avoid people's eyes out of fear they could see how uncomfortable I felt. But Aisha Jenkins smiled at me. So did Kenya. So did Kayla Burnett. "Congratulations," Kayla said.

"What?" I said. "I haven't done anything?!"

I worked my way to the wall where the cast roster was posted. My eyes rose to the top of the piece of paper. The cast was listed from lead and larger roles to ensemble and orchestra and dance corps members. I looked across . . . and saw my name at the very top left. *June Jackson.* My eyes shifted to the right-hand column to see what role I would play. There it was.

DOROTHY

And now I was officially an ACTRESS!!!

I jumped up and down, squealing, unable to control my excitement. I had to let my true feelings loose. My true excitement. I was Dorothy!

"Whaaaaaaaaaaaaaaaaa!!!!" I said, in complete shock. I didn't notice that other people were standing next to me, congratulating me. Candace Brown from seventh grade held her hand up for what seemed like forever before my eyes came into focus enough to realize she was trying to give me a high five. "I can't believe it!" I said. *Oh my gosh!*

The Wiz! Cast

"Girl, believe it," Candace said. "Rehearsals start in January, after winter break."

Just as I turned to go to my first class, Alvin was all of a sudden beside me. "Okay, June! I told you."

"Oh my gosh, Alvin, um, hi, thank you!" I stammered.

"I'm your Scarecrow," he said. "Because I reminded Mrs. Stevens so much of Michael Jackson."

"I bet you did!" I said. "Wow, looks like we're going to be rehearsing right after break."

My thoughts and my mouth were running on high. "Hey, if you ever want to run lines together we could rehearse at my house over the holidays."

"Yeah, all right," Alvin said. "Let's do it."

He smiled as he stuck his fist out for a fist bump. I returned the gesture. My cheeks burned from smiling. Dorothy. Wow! This was indeed a brand-new day for June Naomi Jackson . . . America's next big breakout star!

✦

I went to my locker singing along to the music playing inside my head. I couldn't believe the legendary Diana Ross and I were going to have something in common: leading roles in major productions! I basically floated on air to homeroom. I knew I was supposed to wait for Nia and Olive like usual, but I was so excited I just went straight there. I was relieved when I saw them sitting in the first two rows already.

"I got it!" I squealed. "I'm Dorothy. I. Am. Dorothy!"

Olive excitedly clasped her hands "OMG, June, that's so exciting! We have to celebrate! This is so big! Congratulations!" She reached out her arms. "Come here!" We excitedly hugged.

Nia sat back in her seat, looking more surprised than happy for me.

"Girl, reeeeeeally?" she said, like a low-key drawn-out question, as if she doubted that I could score the lead role. "Well, okay?! I had no idea you had it in you but, wow, like, get it!"

"I think that was a congratulations?" I replied, the sarcasm in my voice rising. "I couldn't tell if one of my best friends for life was ACTUALLY happy for me there."

"Yes, girl, of course! What, you think I'm not happy for you? This is big, June! Like, really big!"

"I know!" I said. "I mean, I've only been studying *The Wiz* for, like, ever. But wow, I never thought I'd get the lead role!"

“Me neither,” Nia said. “But I guess since Ayanna Pullman got cast in this season of *Queen Sugar,* she wasn’t available. So they went with the next best thing.”

I was too excited to let the shade of that comment kill my happiness.

“What’s the deal with costumes and stuff? Will you have to change your hair or anything for the role? Because Diana Ross had that short Afro in the movie.”

“I don’t know,” I said with a shrug.

“Like, the hair was *real* short,” Nia continued. “Have you ever had your hair short?”

“Yeah,” I said. “Like when I was three. Hair grows back, though. I’ll do whatever I need to for the role.” Where was this train of conversation going? It’s just hair!

“What about wardrobe, though?” Nia continued, finally perking up. She was literally more excited about the potential wardrobe than me scoring the lead role. “That whole movie was mad seventies chic! Bell bottoms! Large collars! And Diana Ross’s classic pastel girly look! Do you think you’re gonna need a wardrobe person? Maybe I should volunteer my services.”

“I thought you hated the theater,” I said, and scrunched my eyebrows.

“I don’t like phony people *in* theater,” Nia clarified, twirling a braid around her finger. “But wardrobe is something I love, and you know that I'm good at it. But"—Nia's mood changed, as if she was scared she looked too eager to join *The Wiz* after being so against it during lunch the other day—"whatever, basketball season is starting anyway, so I'll probably be too busy."

Why oh why does everything Nia says have to come with a side of shade? I thought to myself. I almost wanted to not tell Nia anything more about *The Wiz*. If she was going to keep hating on the entire production, then why even bother sharing my happiness with her?

"Anyway," Olive said, keeping the mood light. "We're so proud of you, June."

"All right, homeroom, let's get settled for attendance," Mrs. Worth said. Nia quickly turned to the front of the classroom. Olive gave me one last smile before turning toward Mrs. Worth. I smiled back at both of them, but I was really bothered by Nia's reaction. Had she really doubted that I could get the leading role in the play? What kind of a friend was she? I thought my best friend was supposed to be there to cheer me on, to encourage me. But she just wanted to mock me. Mock my dreams. Spit on something that fueled a creative spark in me. I felt the rage bubbling inside my chest—I was going to explode at Nia if I didn't get this down somewhere stat.

I pulled out my school tablet and brought up my blog. My fingers typed quickly:

CONFESSION #65:

Hello?! Did my best friend Nia not hear me tell her that I got the lead role of Dorothy in *The Wiz*? She seemed more interested in talking about clothes than congratulating me for getting the role of Dorothy! Like, is she not happy for me? Is she jealous of me? Jealous that I'm going to be, like, this big famous actress and she probably wouldn't even get the role of a Munchkin? Maybe she's just not made for the stage like I am! I mean, she would make a good stylist, no doubt about that. Maybe that's what she's meant to be, while I'm made to be a star! She just lost her invite to accompany me to the Oscars when I'm nominated for

"June," Nia said unexpectedly over my shoulder. I almost dropped my tablet on the ground.

"WHAT, GIRL? DANG! You scared me."

Nia jumped back. She looked down at me and raised an eyebrow. "Whatcha writing there? Must be important if you missed the bell."

My cheeks got warm again. Did Nia see what I was writing? Did she know that I had a secret blog where I put all the truths I was keeping from the world? Oh man, after all, she and Chloe were the only ones who knew about the spell!

"I—um . . ."

"Type fast, we gotta go to our next class," she said, and slinked off.

I shook my head as I watched her go. If she'd read

anything I had just typed, there was no doubt we'd get into a huge fight—way bigger than whatever petty stuff she'd been pulling the last few weeks. I looked back at my tablet and checked the time. I had about thirty more seconds to jot down my feelings before I had to run to my next class. I typed super fast, making crazy spelling mistakes along the way:

Anywhoo . . . me. DOrothy! The lead role in this play! 🤩 Just like Mom was back in the daY. I am so excited . . . and I . . . have to tell my dadd now . . .

Oooooooofffff!!!

Okay, I gotta think this thru. I got the the bigggest role. He shuld be happy about thAT, right? And since I got the lead part, then my change of being a famous and succesful actrss in the real wrld—in Hollywoood!—would be pritty great, too! Mayb I start acting FIRst, then cross over to directin, or writin? Or producing? I could be the next Marsai Martin! And then HE could be my date to the Oscars once I'm nomininated, in stead of Nia! See, Me being in the school musical is puttin me on a path toward becommming successful! And that's what DAd wants for me anyway. So, doesn't erevybody win? They could win—if I could get up the nrve to just tell the man I'm IN the play. Arrggghh!

CHAPTER TEN

I was beaming like a light bulb all day in school. Nothing could dim my mood. *No one* could dim my mood.

I was stoked to tell my mother about the play when she came to pick me up after school. "All right! My baby's gonna be a star!" she said in the car ride home. "Your father's going to be so proud!"

Well, *almost* nothing could dim my mood. "Mom!" I said. "Really?" Already? It was too soon! We hadn't even started rehearsals!

"Honey, you said you'd wait until the audition! You got it! Now it's time to tell him."

I closed my eyes tightly. I didn't want to have the

conversation with Dad only to have him throw dirt all over my new passion.

"I'll get on it," I mumbled, with every intention of waiting as long as I could possibly wait before telling him.

We pulled into the garage, and I beelined for my room. I dropped my book bag on the floor and flopped on my bed. Maybe I wouldn't have to tell Dad about the musical tonight. Was there any chance he could get held up in court tonight? And tomorrow night? And the night after?

Just then the ceiling seemed to shift. Then a small piece of dirt fell from the ceiling onto my forehead. Maybe it was plaster? I wiped it off. Then another piece floated onto my cheek. And another one. Then I realized it wasn't plaster when the air got hazier and hazier, and the sprinkles of white matter became thicker and started to swirl into a funnel at the foot of my bed.

After a minute or two, the funnel cloud of dust settled, and Victoria appeared out of thick air.

She coughed a couple of times as she smoothed her dress down. "June! Well, well! Exciting stuff today! Congratulations on getting the lead role!"

I wiped dust away from my face. "Um, thanks."

"You followed your true desire to audition and you went for it, and you got it!" Victoria said. "See what good happens when you do things that make you happy and not just things that make other people happy? I saw you during your audition—it was like true joy beamed through your body as you sang. Following your truth got you the leading role!"

I put a hand on my heart. "I would like to think that it was my stellar acting ability and Broadway-level vocals that got me the role, but okay, yeah, the truth has helped."

"Well, of course, your talent helped, too, but you wouldn't have found your real talents had you not found your truth," Victoria said. "So, now that you've landed the role, you have to tell your father. You have been stalling on telling him about the play. Why, darling?"

"I didn't want to tell him before I auditioned, because

what would be the point of that?" I said. "What if I didn't make it?"

Victoria took a seat on the edge of my bed. "That's no longer a worry. Now it's time to tell him. Tonight is a very good time to do that."

I started pacing around my bedroom floor. I felt a headache coming on. My mouth suddenly turned dry and mealy, like I'd eaten a handful of cornmeal. "Well, what if, like, I got the part on a fluke? What if the director of the show decided they'd made a mistake casting me in the lead role when I had no experience?" I spoke doubly fast. "What if I totally flopped onstage the first week of rehearsals and they kicked me out of the show? And then I'd have to admit I'd been a complete and total and utter failure, and that I'd failed at acting and singing of all things!"

"June. Breathe!" Victoria said. "You got the part. It's yours. You're not going to flop. What you are going to do is tell your dad."

"Listen, I'll do it, on my own time," I said.

Victoria's tone turned serious. "Let me remind you that this spell means you tell the truth at all times, no matter how scared you are of other people's reactions. It means not hiding the truth from others, or yourself. Besides, remember that heart-to-heart talk you had with your father where he told you about his desire to create a legacy for you? The great success he sees in you?"

She stood tall in front of me, and glitter fell from her shoulders. "I'm going to up the ante on our little challenge. If you don't tell your father you're starring in this play soon, I can guarantee that opening night in your first major actress role will not be as successful as you hope."

I gasped. "You wouldn't dare do anything to make me mess up!" I said. "This has been one of the biggest things to ever happen to me of all time! You wouldn't do anything to ruin that, would you? That's not very fairy godmotherly of you!"

Victoria put her hand on my shoulder. "Darling, I want nothing more than for you to succeed in this play. I wouldn't do anything to jeopardize that. But you must learn that you cannot keep hiding the truth from people. You have to tell your father that you're starring in the play. I can't lift the spell unless you tell him. I will be watching."

Victoria backed away from the bed and started spinning in a tight circle until a swirl of fairy dust surrounded her. A funnel cloud formed faster and faster in front of me until she disappeared into thin air once again. Twinkles of matter in front of my eyes reminded me of her recent presence. I flopped back onto the bed and closed my eyes. My chest tightened up, like someone was giving me a bear hug from behind. My mind started racing. What was I going to do?

✦

We were just finished setting up dinner when Dad came home (nope, he hadn't gotten held up in court after all, drat). "Baby girl, how you doing?" he asked as he gave me a kiss on the cheek and put his briefcase down. I smiled nervously. "Be right back, gotta get out of these work clothes," he said.

Grilled lime chicken skewers with a side of rice and roasted veggies were steaming hot and on the table when he came back down. I took my seat and watched as Dad came back into the room and took a seat at the table as well. What was I going to tell him? *How* was I going to tell him? Was Mom going to slip and say something first?

My stomach tensed up. I bit my lower lip. I started humming the words to "Ease on Down the Road" to myself to divert my racing mind from my dad's potential reaction. "MM mm mm, MM mm, mm, MMMMmmmmmmmm."

My head automatically fell into a quiet bopping rhythm as I mumble-sang to myself. My breathing slowed, my stomach relaxed. I felt calm again. Goodness, *The Wiz* was good for my soul.

We began to assemble food on our plates. "Oops, forgot extra pepper," Mom said, rising from the table briefly.

"So, what's up at school, June? Good day today?"

I silent hummed to myself. "Yep, all good."

My mom looked at me. She was ready for me to spill

the beans about the musical. But I sure wasn't. "I want extra lime wedges," I announced, then went back into the kitchen to find them. I came back a few minutes later with limes.

Then I drank my water real fast. Suddenly I had to get up again. "Excuse me, I have to use the restroom," I said. The more I was away from the table, the fewer opportunities I had to tell my dad about the musical. Now I was literally running from the truth.

I came back to the table. My dad turned to me. "June, what happened at school today?"

I looked at him, then looked down at my lap. "Oh, I gotta grab a napkin. The chicken is sticky!" I said. I got up again, and slowly found another napkin, and reorganized our linens drawer while I was there. Dad was talking about something else with Mom now. Phew! I came back to the table.

"You guys hear about that actress from that sitcom you all watch on Netflix?" Dad said as I sat back down. "Filed for bankruptcy. Seems after taxes she couldn't afford her brand-new condo downtown. Told you Hollywood doesn't pay."

My mother looked at me. I looked at her. Neither of us said anything.

I felt a tightness in my stomach. This was the reason why I didn't want to tell Dad about acting. He never talks

about the many actresses around here who *are* successful, who have bought condos and can afford their cars and do have health insurance, just like he does. I had to tell him that I could be one of those actresses, that the school had already spotted my acting ability and cast me as the lead role in *The Wiz*!

"Follow your truth," Victoria would say to me. In fact, she was saying it right now. I could hear a little voice over my shoulder saying, "Follow your truth. Tell him."

"Not all actresses go bankrupt, honey," my mom said. "Right, June?"

"I'm not saying that," Dad said. "But it's an unstable life." He took another piece of chicken. "Whatever, no need to worry about that anyway, right, June?"

I felt a flutter in my nose. It was as if someone had sprinkled extra pepper on my chicken. A lot of pepper. I had to sneeze.

"Achoooo! Achooo-achooo!"

I cleared my throat a few times, but my throat still felt scratchy and raw. I dabbed away at my nose while cursing Victoria's name for sprinkling my dinner with fairy dust, turning me into a sneezy, wheezy mess. Flustered, I eked out the only thing I could think to say in the moment: "Maybe?"

"Anyway, let's talk about the holidays," my dad said, changing the subject and turning toward my mom. "Baby, you think we should head up to the lake this year or celebrate here?"

My mom unlocked her gaze from my eyes and turned to Dad. They fell deeper into conversation about the holidays and potential trips and visitors, while I quietly ate my chicken and rice. I let the adults talk, hoping they'd forget all about the wannabe actress child at the table. Victoria had a good thing going. Being invisible in this case would sit just fine with me.

CONFESSION #69:

Maybe if I practice how Dad will react to me being in the play, I can deal with it:

Me: "Dad, I have big news. I'm going to be an actress!"

Dad: "Uh, no, you're gonna get a real job first."

Me: "Daddy, guess what? I'm such a great actress that I scored the lead role in the school musical! I'm going to be Dorothy in *The Wiz*!"

Dad: *(Blank stare. Then his head explodes.)*

Me: "Daddy, guess what? I'm going to play one of America's classic leading roles! I'm going to be Dorothy in *The Wiz*! At just eleven years old I scored a role Diana Ross got in her thirties! I'm a theater prodigy!"

Dad: "If you were a prodigy, you'd be working in Hollywood already. Besides, did Diana Ross have health insurance when she was thirty?"

Sigh.

CHAPTER ELEVEN

Holiday break had just begun, and Christmas was a few days away. It was chilly outside, and in between shifts at the hospital, Mom had baked batches of shortbread and candy cane sugar cookies for neighbors and coworkers. I had put in a request for three different types of chocolate chip cookies. Our oven seemed to be on 24-7.

Alvin decided to make good on my offer to rehearse, and he texted me to see if he could come over this afternoon. My mom was home from the hospital today, so we made a plan to meet.

When I came down for breakfast, I knew Dad would be downstairs already, drinking his coffee, reading the paper, ready to ask me about my day's schedule. Every time I was in front of Dad it was an opportunity to tell him about the musical. I knew this, and my mom knew this, too. I tried to delay my departure from my room as late as I could, but this morning I was starving and there were cinnamon rolls on the kitchen counter calling my name. I loved the holidays.

Mom was standing near the refrigerator, pouring a glass of juice, while Dad sat at the kitchen table, typing something into his phone. "Hey, sweetheart, what's going on?" he asked. "Vacay all day, right?"

"Same ol' same ol', Dad," I said, growing slightly more anxious with every word. I could feel my mom's eyes boring into me. I looked nervously at her. She gave me a wink—a knowing wink, a wink that said, "I just know you're going to do me proud and tell your father that you're starring in *The Wiz* at school, right?"

I said nothing as I beelined for the cinnamon rolls on the counter and reached around my mom for the almond milk. She watched my every move. I looked down at my glass as I poured the milk, then carried my plate and glass to the kitchen table and sat down next to Dad.

"June, what are your plans today, dear?" Mom said, looking right at me. I jerked my head up from my plate, staring at her, searching for empathy. *Please, Mom, don't make me do this right now. I really don't want to anger him at breakfast.*

“I was hoping Alvin could come over,” I asked.

“Alvin?” Dad asked. “Haven’t heard that name in a while.”

“Yeah, he wanted to show me . . . something he’s working on,” I said. That wasn’t a lie. Okay, it was a half lie. I felt the sneeze coming right away.

“He’s a nice kid. Audrey, you’ll be here?”

“Yes, dear.”

“All right, I’ll see you all later.” Dad got up and picked up his keys. He didn’t show much concern about why Alvin was coming over, thank God. My nose itched more. I turned and looked as my dad continued walking out the

door to the garage. Phew! He was gone. I took a bite of my cinnamon roll in relief.

Just when I thought the coast was clear, a large burst of cinnamon powder floated up into my nose and caused me to sneeze out a chunk of icing-covered sugary dough. *Aah-choo!* The ball of dough flew back onto my plate. Dang it, Victoria! Again with the flying food!

"You got lucky, June," Mom said threateningly.

"I swear I'll tell him! Next time!"

"Don't drag this out, June. You only have a few more chances. I'm not keeping the truth from your father, so if you don't tell him, I will. And he won't like that I had to be the one to tell him and not you."

I clenched my teeth. "Mom, I got it. I'll tell him."

She got up to walk toward the den. The last thing I wanted was for Mom to spring this news on Dad herself. I wanted to be the one to tell him . . . when I was ready. Maybe he'd be more convinced this was a good thing for me if he could see my face as I told him. I called out to her. "Mom? Promise you won't tell him? I'll do it," I said, my forehead crinkling. She nodded, then went into the den.

I popped another piece of cinnamon roll in my mouth and chewed away my anxiety. Sweet bread and sugary icing can spark joy even in the biggest worrywart. But even the tastiest holiday treat wasn't going to get me out of this mess.

✦

Alvin came over in the afternoon with his laptop. He usually carried a laptop or tablet or some sort of electronic on him because he liked coding and games, so this wasn't surprising to me. "Hey, Dorothy," he said jokingly. I didn't mind the nickname.

"Hey, Scarecrow," I said. "You been practicing how to ease on down the road?"

"Of course," he said. Then, he shook his right leg as he hopped on the other leg, moving farther down the hallway and into my house. "Don't break nothing!" I called out.

We sat in the living room, watching clips of *The Wiz* and going over various scenes. Alvin sang a few bars of "The Crow Anthem" *("You can't win . . . you can't break even . . .")*. Alvin's voice sounded smooth, buttery.

"You learned to sing like that in church?"

"Yup," he said.

"You're really good."

"Well, thanks, but I'm no Michael Jackson."

We played out the scene where Dorothy meets Scarecrow for the first time. Alvin knew all his lines already. I looked into his pained eyes as he showed me the top of his head, pretending to reveal that he didn't have a brain. Then we danced around the living room, running through the scene, laughing, holding hands, and cheering as we went into "Ease on Down the Road."

I smiled and laughed with Alvin. His smile was warm and genuine but also perfect for the stage. I forgot about everything else around us while we rehearsed. I didn't even notice that my mother was watching us when we pretended to dance down the yellow brick road.

Two hours had already gone by when my mom finally interrupted us—I hadn't even been checking the time, we were having so much fun. "Ahem, Alvin, your mother's outside."

"Wow, time just flew by," Alvin said.

"Yeah," I said, my heart fluttering. "That was fun!"

"You're a bomb Dorothy, June," he said, smiling.

I blushed—the same way I did when Lee sometimes brushed up against my arm or said something that made me snort-laugh. I covered my face with my hand to hide my rosy cheeks.

"Thanks," I mumbled. "So, yeah, should we, like, do this again soon?"

"Yeah!" he said. "I'll text you."

He opened the door and dashed out to his mom's car. I closed the front door quickly so he couldn't see me smiling and blushing so embarrassingly hard.

HONEST June

CONFESSION #82:

Alvin is an amazing singer. And actor. And dancer. He really helps put me at ease when I'm going through my lines, too—he's such a natural. It's a big responsibility to play Dorothy in *The Wiz.* And I really want to do well. Before he came over, I was super nervous. But Alvin made me feel light. This role feels easy when I'm working with him, and we haven't even done real rehearsals yet! I really hope we end up rehearsing a lot together.

And how have I not known that Alvin was such a great singer? Maybe 'cause I've spent so much time with Lee and Olive and Nia . . . But maybe I should spend less time with Lee and more time with Alvin. Alvin and I have more in common anyway now, because we are, you know, ACTORS. And now that Lee likes Nia maybe they'll spend more time together 😬 . . . and I can spend more time getting to know Alvin. 😊

CHAPTER TWELVE

"Hey, look, it's Diana Ross!" Nia said to me as she walked into my house and handed me a small box on Christmas Eve.

"Very funny," I said, annoyed by her mocking of my newfound interest—but, also, not gonna lie, I did like being compared to one of the greatest superstars of all time.

Olive handed me a small red gift bag. "Happy holidays," she said.

"Thanks, friends!" I replied with a hug. We'd met up to make some holiday cookies and exchange gifts before Christmas Day. The girls followed me toward the kitchen, where Luisa, our housekeeper, was at the sink washing dishes, and we took out the cookie dough and baking sheets.

"These are for you," I said as I handed them their gifts. I'd bought them both peppermint hand lotion and mini manicure kits, figuring they could use them after we got our hands dirty making the cookies.

"How's prepping for the play?" Olive asked.

"It's a lot of work already and we haven't even officially started rehearsals! I have a lot of lines to memorize," I explained. "But it's really exciting. And the seventh and eighth graders have been really nice to me so far—they've

sent me a couple of emails and Instagram DMs congratulating me."

"That's nice," Nia said. "So there's no jealousy among the cast, like from older kids who might have thought they should have gotten the part above you?" she asked. She raised her eyebrow. Was she trying to tell me something?

I felt myself getting defensive. "Well, there's no jealousy on this ensemble." Which was true . . . at least so far.

"Good," Nia said, and I swore she rolled her eyes as she turned away. "Well, you missed out on a lot of things going on with us."

"Like what? What have I missed?" Had they been hanging out without me again?! Had they been talking behind my back while they hung out? Had Nia been trash-talking my acting abilities to Olive? I blinked repeatedly, frustrated.

"Well, you know, lots been going on with us, like . . . you know, stuff . . ."

"You haven't missed a thing, June, I don't know what Nia's talking about," Olive chimed in with a smile and a shrug. "It's holiday break, nothing's going on." Then why had Nia made it sound like I was missing out on all this amazing stuff? Like they had been bouncing from mall to mall and ice-skating and rocking around the Christmas tree without me? We had a group text that basically tracked all of our whereabouts because we were always in touch, so I liked to think I knew exactly where they'd been—home, maybe the grocery store, and maybe one trip to the mall. Was Nia just trying to annoy me? Was this what happened when actors finally got their big break—their friends that weren't so big got jealous?

"Great, so let's make some stuff happen tonight!" I joked and forced a huge laugh.

Nia opened the cookie dough package and mixed in extra chocolate chips. She started spooning small balls onto the baking sheet.

"How's Alvin so far?" she asked. "He's gonna be the Scarecrow, right? Can he really sing?"

"Yeah!" I said. "He came over the other day and we rehearsed." My voice got higher in pitch and I found myself speaking twice as fast. "He sounds just like Michael Jackson did in the movie. I was so surprised. His voice! And there was this one scene where we have to dance down the yellow brick road and he can really dance, too. And he said I made a great Dorothy."

"Riiiiight," Nia said. "Alvin's got you very excited, June."

"What? No!" I said. Suddenly I felt an itch in my nose. Was I excited? "I'm just saying he's a good actor."

"We got it, girl," Nia said, smiling. "Alvin is your Scarecrow. You and Alvin, following that yellow brick road, wink wink." She scooped the final cookie dough ball onto the sheet. Luisa helped us put it in the oven.

"Anyway, what's up with Lee?" Nia said, quickly changing the subject. "Is he, like, building stuff?"

Oh no, the dreaded Lee topic. No matter how slowly we got to me admitting the truth, it was for sure going to end uncomfortably, and I couldn't put it off any longer. It was going to have to happen soon—if not now. I paused and took a breath. "He's helping build the set, yes," I said.

"Like, what part of the set?"

"Like, you know how the Scarecrow is on the farm, so he's building farm stuff, and the yellow brick road, and Oz! I haven't seen him much since the break started."

I felt warm. Maybe it was because the oven was on? Or because I knew I should admit to Nia that Lee wants to hang out with her. I needed to just say it. The longer I held it in, the more uncomfortable I felt. It was making me feel sick to hold in the truth in front of Nia.

"June's always had a thing for Lee, but she just won't admit it," Nia said to Olive, and smiled with one corner of her mouth.

I stammered and started to sweat. It felt like my throat was swelling up. I certainly didn't want to release the deep yet super top-secret feelings I had for my friend that made me blush and fidget. But I had to tell the truth. I was sweating—why was it so hot in here? Did Luisa turn the oven temperature up? Victoria! Dang it! *Okay. Here goes.*

"Well . . . um . . . well, no that's not . . . ," I said. I felt a rush of words coming up to my throat. I had to get out the truth. At least telling the truth about Lee wanting to hang out with Nia would help me keep quiet about my secret crush on Lee. To protect my feelings, I could tell Nia about Lee's real feelings. I was still telling the truth either way—and maybe Victoria would acknowledge it and release me out of this spell! "Anyway, I'm like hyper-focused on this play now, and . . . I think . . . you know . . . Lee, may, like, might be feeling *you* now."

"What do you mean? Did he say something about me?" Nia said eagerly, leaning forward over the counter with a spoon in hand.

"Well, he said he wanted to hang out with you," I said.

"He did? When? Hang out with me when? Where? Tell me!"

I shoved a dozen loose chocolate chips in my mouth, then a half dozen more, hoping that if I kept my mouth full of chocolate, I wouldn't be able to spill all the details about the bike ride and Lee's confession weeks ago. But now that I had broken the news, I had to tell the entire story.

I felt a sneeze coming on. Of course Victoria wouldn't let this moment pass without forcing me to give a true

confessional. I tried to fight the urge to sneeze, but the itching increased, like I'd just inhaled a super-fuzzy cat up my nose, and all of a sudden my face crinkled and I let out a huge *aaaachhoooooo!!!* . . . along with a mouthful of chocolate chips, which came shooting out of my mouth across the kitchen, almost hitting Olive.

"Girl, be careful!" Nia said. "Are you taking anything for those allergies?"

"No . . . Like I said, Lee told me that he wanted to hang out with you the last time we took a bike ride." I took a breath and continued. "Before Thanksgiving."

Nia looked at me, surprised. "That was, like, weeks ago. And you didn't say anything?"

"I was waiting until you came over on Black Friday."

"But you didn't tell me then," Nia said. She looked confused.

"I—I didn't know how to bring it up," I stammered.

"But it's been like a month!" Nia said. "Why haven't you told me this? We could have made plans to hang out over winter break! We could have all gone shopping together or gone ice-skating in the town square!"

"I . . . um . . . yes . . . we could have. . . . And we still can! Lee would like that," I said.

Nia's eyes narrowed. She jerked her head back as if she'd just figured out the solution to a complex math problem. "Oh, I know what this is. I know what this is."

I started to blink hard. "What, it's not anything! I just didn't know how to bring it up. It was a few weeks ago and I, um, didn't think about it much since then," I said.

Aaachhoooo! Aaaaaachhoooo! I sneezed. That was a lie. I had thought about how to talk about this pretty much every moment I wasn't thinking about *The Wiz*.

Nia's face turned cold as she slowly backed away from the counter. "Lee is your best guy friend. You've known each other basically since birth, and you know you've had a crush on him for a long time now, even though you're too shy to admit it. You of all people would know if he had feelings for some other girl. And now he finally admits to you that he wants to hang out with me and you get scared. So you just don't tell me. Because you're jealous!"

"That's not true!" I said, panicking. But I knew it was. My stomach started to gurgle. The itch in my nose felt like sandpaper on my sinuses by now. "I just . . . I just didn't think . . . I didn't . . ."

I knew Victoria was going to come out of nowhere somehow and smack me with fairy dust and make me sneeze like a hyena with hay fever and totally embarrass me in front of Nia and Olive any minute now. I tried to hedge my bets with her and jump in with some kind of truth.

"Okay!" I admitted. "I guess I knew about it and

thought about it, but I figured I should stay out of it. I figured he would eventually bring it up to you himself."

Nia stared at me blankly. She pushed into the swinging door, walking out of the kitchen and toward the front door. Her feet made hard stomping sounds with each step, loud enough to wake the dead. I knew this was not going to end well. I followed her down the front hall, desperate to stop her from leaving—if she left, who knew if we could fix it?

"Girl, I cannot believe you," Nia said as she stomped. "You just wanted Lee to yourself, so you didn't even tell

me he asked about me. You're supposed to be my BFF! That's so not cool, June."

Nothing I said at this point, especially if I confessed the full truth, was going to change Nia's mind about how this had gone down. I tried to push words out of my mouth, but nothing would come out.

She grabbed her coat and put on her shoes. "You of all people should've known to tell me the truth," Nia said coldly. "I know you can't lie, because of that spell or whatever that fairy lady put on you in that fun house. All I know is you must have been working extra hard to keep this from me because of it. I'm out. And don't bother texting or calling."

HONEST June

CONFESSION #89:

I hid the truth from my two best friends. Yes, it was a bad thing to do. No, it won't help me get Victoria's spell canceled. But I . . . don't know. Lee and I have known each other since, like, forever. We spend every summer together. Nia doesn't even know what his favorite food is (cheese). I'm the one who's already met Chadwick! Yes, I should've told them. I would want her to tell me if somebody had a crush on me.

This is bad. Awful. Now Nia is going to talk to Lee and tell him what I did and I'm going to look like the worst friend ever—the worst PERSON ever! Now I'm going to be the third wheel and they'll start hanging out and riding bikes together and getting ice cream and he'll never come over for Sunday dinner or jump on my trampoline ever again. And Nia will only want to hang out with Lee and never have any time for me. And I will be alone. Forever. Just me and my laptop and my dolls. 🤤

Unless Alvin wants to hang out . . . 😏

CHAPTER THIRTEEN

A few days after Christmas, I invited Blake, Olive, and Nia over for a holiday sleepover—even though Nia was still massively upset with me. I wanted us all to get together, and I wanted Mom to bake another round of her special chocolate chip cookies for us. Olive and Blake took very little convincing to come over. Even though Olive had family in town, she still made time to come over. "I want to help you and Nia get back on track," Olive said. Always the peacemaker.

But Nia hadn't texted or called since the Lee drama went down in my kitchen. She didn't even wish me a merry Christmas or thank me for her gift. I didn't blame her. She was probably hanging out with Lee every day since our blowup, cursing my name. Wishing I'd literally break a leg in the school musical and not be able to come back to school for the rest of the school year.

I called Nia the morning of the sleepover to check in.

"I'm studying," she said.

Nia never turned down an invitation to a social gathering, much less a social gathering with Olive and me, much less a social gathering with Olive and me during winter break. "Studying?" I asked. "On a Friday night?"

"I have some catching up to do," she said. "Basketball started right before break, and I need to squeeze in studying when I can."

"Riiight," I said slowly. "It's just . . ." I tried to choose my words carefully. "It's winter break."

"Well, that doesn't mean I don't need to get my work done. I still get good grades, June. I'm a pretty smart girl." Nia sounded defensive.

"I didn't say you weren't!" I said. I thought up a few nice things to say to her, to both make her feel good and get her to warm up to me. "You're smart and pretty and so cool," I said, then gritted my teeth—"which is why Lee likes you so much."

Nia let out the kind of short laugh you release when you really don't find a comment funny. She knew, ironically, that I was telling the truth, but it was probably too little too late. "Lee. Right, Lee."

"Well, listen, a sleepover isn't a sleepover without you. Please, please, please, come hang out with us? You can bring your books with you, too."

"I'll pass," Nia said, then hung up.

I shook my head. Not telling the truth about Lee and her as soon as I knew it had created beef between Nia and me so big, she'd rather study than hang out with me. How long could she stay mad at me? Would she not speak to me all winter break? Or the entire spring semester? Was this the end of our friendship?

I tried to shake off the Nia call and get ready for the sleepover with my friends. I went to my closet to look for my favorite holiday pajamas, the same ones I'd been wearing all week, which would likely have holes in them by New Year's Eve from wearing them so much. I dug them out of a pile of clean clothes I meant to fold and put away today, but hadn't gotten around to yet.

Just then, I saw a cloud of matter floating in the closet. It grew thicker, like a spiderweb, then swirled around in a funnel cloud. The tornado in the middle of my closet signaled the arrival of my one and only fairy godmother. *Victoria.*

She emerged from the funnel cloud and stepped out of my closet. She cleared her throat and smoothed her gown. "June, June, June," she said.

I knew exactly what she was going to say.

"See what happens when you don't tell the truth right away?"

"Yeah, I get it, Victoria," I said, annoyed. "I didn't tell Nia about Lee being interested in her, and now she's mad. So how about instead of berating or punishing me, will you help me get my friendship back? What truth can I tell her to help make things better between us again?"

"Why don't you tell her how you honestly feel about Lee?"

My voice rose a few decibels. "Because I don't know how I honestly feel about Lee! And why do I have to tell everyone everything! Can't I keep some feelings to myself? I can tell the truth without sharing every little personal detail about my private life, can't I?"

"Of course," Victoria said. "But when you have been directly asked questions, like when Nia asked you if Lee liked her, that's different. Remember, I can't lift the spell if you're not telling the truth."

I closed my eyes and slumped back on the floor in front of my bed. Victoria waved her magic wand above her head, and fairy dust rained down around her. She took a few spins around until the dust covered her completely, and in a poof she was gone once again.

✦

Olive had arrived at my house first, already wearing her pajamas. She brought a platter of homemade chocolatey brownies.

My mom was in the kitchen gathering a fresh batch of Christmas cookies and some leftover holiday popcorn for the gang. "Hi, Dr. Jackson," Olive greeted her as we walked in. "I know these aren't part of the four food groups, but they're homemade."

"Hi, Olive," Mom said. "Chocolate is a major food group at Christmastime. Thank you, dear."

Olive turned back to me. "Is Nia coming?" she asked.

"Nope," I said, a bit defeated. "She says she has to 'study.' "

The doorbell rang again, and Blake was standing on the porch wearing jeans and a sweatshirt. Olive followed behind me to greet her. "Hey, girl! Where's your pj's?"

"In my bag here," Blake said. "I didn't know we were wearing them to dinner, too."

"No worries," I said. "I live in these things now. They're not coming off until school starts again."

Blake came inside and walked shoulder to shoulder with Olive as they followed me to the living room. Blake complimented Olive on her shoes, and Olive complimented Blake on her braided bracelet she was wearing. These two friends could get along without any drama. Like they'd known each other for years, or at least like they cared enough to be kind to one another for my sake! On the other hand, Nia's and Blake's dads worked together, and Nia couldn't even be bothered to be polite toward Blake. She couldn't even be bothered to show up to this sleepover with us, either. Couldn't we all just get along like one big peaceful pack of American Girl dolls?

"Where's your bathroom again so I can get into my pj's?" Blake asked. I pointed to a door around the corner, and Blake disappeared to get changed.

Blake, Olive, and I had just settled on the living room floor in front of the TV when Dad walked into the living

room carrying his briefcase, returning from work. "Well, hello, girls! Is this an official meeting?"

"No, Dad! Just a sleepover."

"Well, every sleepover needs pizza," he said, putting down his briefcase. Should I order one?" We nodded enthusiastically.

Halfway into our TV show, I got up to grab my cell phone from my room, and as I was walking back toward the living room, I heard my dad ask Blake about field hockey.

"So will you be playing field hockey next year?" he asked Blake. "You guys played well this season. Only one loss!"

"Yep, I'll be on the team next year," Blake said. "I'm on a summer team, too. But before then, it's all about the school musical."

I entered the room just as she said the word "musical." I gritted my teeth. *Please don't mention my name, please don't tell Dad that I'm in* The Wiz, I wished to myself. *He'll be so angry I didn't tell him earlier, and disappointed I am doing yet another thing to not be a lawyer. He'll cancel all future sleepovers so I can "buckle down" and focus on a "real career"!* I took a big inhale as I repeated those words to myself, and my chest felt tight.

"There's a musical?" Dad asked.

I quickly interrupted them. "Hey, guys! So what movie are we watching first?" I said, trying to change the subject.

"Did you know Blake's in the school musical, June?" Dad asked, unbothered by my attempt to distract him.

I kept my eyes focused on the TV screen, glaring at the holiday movies available on Netflix. My mouth was getting dry. My nose twitched. I felt an itch like a sneeze was coming on. I stammered, "Yeah . . . uh, yes, I did. Blake's a dancer."

"Ah, I see," Dad said.

"Yes," Blake said slowly, then looked at me. I flashed her a look, the look that said, "Don't say any more." I looked at Olive quickly and flashed her the same look. Both froze in their seats.

I felt a stronger itch in my nose. I rubbed it, hoping it would clear. But as the feeling got more intense, I had to sneeze. I held it in. My eyes got watery.

"So, what play is it?" Dad asked.

Blake looked at me and shook her head. "It's *The Wiz*," she said.

"Ah, I love *The Wiz*! June, we've seen that at least a dozen times, right?"

"Um . . . uh, yeah," I said. *Please, no one tell him I'm Dorothy! I just want to tell him myself.* My nose was itchier than ever. I tried to exhale through my nose to clear it. No such luck. I knew that if I didn't tell him, I was about to have the largest sneezing fit ever. "Um . . ." *Here's my chance to confess. Get it out, June!* "Ahhh, ahhhh . . ."

DING-DONG!

"Pizza's here!" my father declared. "Excuse me," he said, dashing to grab his wallet and then answer the door.

"Aaaaahh—*chhoooo*!" I sneezed.

"Bless you!" my dad called from the hallway. The itchy feeling subsided. Blake and Olive looked at me.

"You haven't told him you're starring in the school musical?" Blake looked at me with crinkled eyebrows. "You're the lead! It's a big deal!"

"I know!" I said. "I just want to tell him in my own way."

"All this time you've been working hard to impress him, and you finally have something that's impressive, and you're hiding it!" Olive said. "Tell him! My parents would be so proud if I scored the lead in a musical."

"Your parents appreciate the arts!" I said. "They love Broadway, and, heck, you're in the orchestra! My dad's different. He's not about that creative life."

"How do you know?"

"How do I know? You do recall that I just got off of punishment after telling him I didn't want to be a lawyer. This man believes in careers like law, politics, finance, things that involve degrees and schooling and facts and figures. Acting? Not a career to him."

Dad walked through the room with two large pizza pies. My throat started to get dry, like I was walking through the desert. I hoped that the smell of hot melted cheese and pepperoni would derail my dad's train of thought away from the musical and school and me. It had certainly thrown my attention.

"Mmmm, hot out of the oven! Let's get it, girls," he called out from the kitchen, putting the pizzas on the counter.

No one mentioned *The Wiz* again as we ate slices of pizza and milled around the kitchen. The sneezing feeling was gone, too. A good thing—no one likes snotty pizza. The longer people ate, the less likely it was people would bring up the school musical in conversation. After dinner, my dad went to his office for a bit, and then to bed, while Blake, Olive, and I stayed up late watching movies, browsing the internet, and wishing Nia was there. Just before midnight, the three of us tucked ourselves under blankets on the sofa and fell asleep in front of the television. Nia never answered any of our text messages the entire night.

CHAPTER FOURTEEN

Once winter break was over, rehearsals for *The Wiz* began. We were often broken up into separate groups for chorus, band, dancers, and the lead characters. I had to participate in just about all the scenes, since Dorothy is onstage for basically the entire play, so I had to show up to every rehearsal.

Mrs. Stevens, who was directing our play, wore black shirts and wide-legged pants to every rehearsal and red-rimmed glasses that she shifted from the top of her head to her nose between scenes. She was born in Featherstone Creek, then went to New York to become a Broadway actress, then returned to town to teach English, drama, and the arts at FCMS a few years ago. Every day at the

beginning of rehearsals, precisely at three-fifteen, she clapped her hands loudly three times to grab everyone's attention.

I loved watching the other cast members dance and sing along to all the songs I'd memorized all through winter break. Even when I wasn't in certain scenes, I still danced and mouthed the words to the play along with the cast. I was also quick to help other cast members. Like when Carmen Evans messed up her dance steps during "Brand New Day," I was there to help her. "Carmen! You forgot the steps again! It's one and two, turn and hands!" Mrs. Stevens gave me a glance, then nodded. "Yes, Carmen, she's right. But relax, take a breath, then get into it."

Or when Kevin Thomas, who was playing Tinman, forgot his lines during rehearsal of the scene where Dorothy and Tinman meet for the first time. "That's not what he says!" I blurted out before I fed him his line. "Did you rehearse during winter break?" I asked him, genuinely curious. Kevin seemed a bit embarrassed. But I would be, too, if I forgot my lines.

And when some of the music wasn't perfectly on key when they started up "Ease on Down the Road" for the eighth time that day, I was first to point it out, even if it was just a run-through for music without any of the dancers. I mean, practice makes perfect, and we want the show to be perfect? Right?

✦

"All right, kids, let's tackle our first big dance scene," Mrs. Stevens said. "June, to the front of the stage, please. Alvin, you as well. Let's do 'Ease on Down the Road.'"

I shuffled to my mark on the stage. Alvin met me at his mark. I imagined him in wardrobe with an old mop on his head to make him look like a scarecrow, with loose bits of straw glued onto his long sleeves and pants.

The music kicked on. *"Come on and ease on down, ease on down the road . . . ,"* I sang, dancing to the beat around Alvin, happily smiling as I moved. Alvin was on point. His voice, already in character, quavered as he wobbled from his hunched-over position at the beginning of the song until the found his strength toward the chorus. It was fun. I sang louder. And then I danced more enthusiastically, until . . .

"Wait, hold it here!" Mrs. Stevens said.

What happened? I wondered. I was singing, I knew the song. Did Alvin miss something?

"June," Mrs. Stevens said. "Try to match your emotions to the words. Remember, in the beginning you're supposed to be more concerned that Scarecrow can't find his footing. Be a little more serious, determined to help him. Then you can get lighter and more joyous when he gets stronger. All right, take it from the top, let's go!"

I gave it another go. This time I scrunched my eyebrows together like my dad does whenever I'm in trouble. I barked orders at Alvin. "Come on now! Get on your feet! You can do it! Come on!" I might have gritted my teeth a little too hard. I felt a little pain in my jaw.

"Stop! Stop!" Mrs. Stevens said. I turned toward her. "June, not so harsh. Remember, gently encourage Alvin. Keep it light."

I felt discouraged. I had studied these lines all winter break, but it seems like I was doing too much. How could I possibly be doing too much? I was an actress! I was ACTING. I shook my head as I went back to my mark.

Alvin turned to me. "It's cool, just be natural," he said.

"All right, from the top!" Mrs. Stevens yelled. I gently

put my arms around Alvin, helping him up to his feet. "That's it, you got it," I said. I moved slowly, following Alvin's lead as he wobbled and bobbed in my arms, trying to find his footing and slowly rising up to stand. Then he skipped down the yellow brick road, and I fell in step with him. "That's it, June!" Mrs. Stevens said. "Yes!"

My smile naturally got bigger as Mrs. Stevens cheered us on. We breezed through our lines as the music kicked up and the song came on. Alvin and I sang in tune, dancing and skipping, and Mrs. Stevens started clapping and nodding about halfway through. I felt so light on my feet, I don't know if I really touched the yellow brick road as I danced. I looked at Alvin's face and I just felt like time stood still, like I had no worries about my dad or Nia or the cursed truth-telling spell.

"And YAAAS!" Mrs. Stevens said as the song ended and the scene came to a close. "Great job, guys. Let's go on to the next scene."

✦

Mrs. Stevens was waiting for me after rehearsal. "June, got a minute?" she said.

I took a seat next to her in the front row of the auditorium. "June, great work today," she said. "I just wanted to give you a helpful reminder not to overthink your lines.

You are much more relaxed when you just go with the flow."

My cheeks suddenly felt warm.

"Some actors think they have to be overdramatic because they're onstage, and they feel like they have to be over-the-top. Sometimes less is more."

I felt a heaviness in my chest, like a weight was sinking to my belly. "But don't I have to be lively onstage?"

"Of course, June, but you can be lively without having to be too dramatic. Or critical of your classmates."

I felt annoyed. I mean, was she trying to say I was a bad actress? Was I not as great as the other kids in the play? Was I a bad Dorothy? I had studied all my lines! I sang in tune, and I'd already memorized the majority of my choreography. I felt a need to defend myself. "Well, maybe you think I'm overacting because you're so close to the stage," I said.

"No," Mrs. Stevens said, removing her glasses from her face and gesticulating with them. "I'm saying this because in relation to the rest of the cast, your delivery and pace are a bit off. I'm just giving you helpful feedback so you can be the best Dorothy you can be on the stage."

I took offense at her words. I mean, I knew I had never done this before, but what I did know for sure was that I put my heart and soul into my performance so far and I could tell exactly when other people weren't doing the

same. "I disagree," I said, saying what I truly felt. Knowing Victoria was watching my every move, and knowing she was putting the pressure on me to tell the truth no matter what in all situations, I told Mrs. Stevens the truth. I thought I was defending my efforts to Mrs. Stevens. "Maybe I'm just outshining the rest of the cast."

"June," Mrs. Stevens said, sitting up taller. Her eyeglasses were in one hand, and she started to point them at me. "I'm telling you what you need to do to be a great actress, not just to know your lines and recite them on a stage. I'm thinking about the whole cast working together—not just you."

I bit my lower lip. I was just being honest, but judging by Mrs. Stevens's reaction, perhaps she didn't appreciate my honesty.

"I just want to make sure I do a good job," I countered.

"June, you'll do great," Mrs. Stevens said, leaning back in her chair and placing her glasses on top of her head. "But sometimes less is more. I'll see you tomorrow."

I stood up and walked toward the exit, my very small but eager ego feeling bruised after Mrs. Stevens's feedback. My acting, and my opinion of my acting, didn't seem to be as well received as I intended. Was I disappointing the director already? Did the rest of the cast think I was doing a good job? Did Alvin think I did a good job?

I walked out of rehearsals and toward the exit of school, my brain in overdrive thinking about Mrs. Stevens's critiques, and walked home alone.

I'd almost made it to my street when suddenly the air started to get hazy around me. A cloud of dust formed in front of me, growing thicker and thicker, and I immediately knew that I'd have company on this walk home after all.

"Hello, Victoria," I said just as she started to take form. "What have I done wrong now?" I rolled my eyes.

"Hi, June," Victoria said, smiling. "I actually wanted to

compliment you on how focused you are in this play. I feel like you really found yourself in acting."

I blinked quickly. "Really? Mrs. Stevens didn't think so," I said, and pouted.

"Well, some of your comments to other kids were a bit harsh, and even your comments to Mrs. Stevens were mean, even though she was just trying to give you helpful direction."

I stopped walking and turned to Victoria. "You told me to tell the truth all the time. I truthfully felt she was picking on me because I was better than the rest of the cast." I looked at Victoria. She looked back at me, blankly, and it suddenly hit me. "Actually . . . that sounds ridiculous, doesn't it?"

"A little," Victoria said. "June, she's the director. Her job is to make sure all the actors play well with each other. You might be the star, but you also have to perform well with the rest of your castmates."

My mind flashed back to how the other students performed during rehearsals. I started walking again, this time a bit faster as frustration bubbled up in my belly again. "But Carmen never gets the dance steps perfect!"

"June, everyone makes mistakes. You're not meant to be perfect yet. That's why it's called rehearsal."

"But why am I wrong when I point out their mistakes? What happened to telling the truth and nothing but?"

Victoria took a few steps in front of me and stopped so I couldn't rush ahead of her. "You mean like how you told your mom her brussels sprouts weren't great? That didn't go over too well, right? There's telling the truth, and then there's *how* you tell the truth. You can tell the truth without sounding mean or insensitive."

"But sometimes the truth hurts," I said. "Like my dad. He's so anticulture! He truly doesn't think acting or writing or anything that doesn't involve thirty years of schooling is a real job! And Nia! That girl *is* boy crazy! First Alvin and now Lee? And Lee liking Nia—doesn't that prove he has horrible taste in girls?!"

"June," Victoria said, shaking her head. "Remember how you told your dad about you not wanting to be a lawyer? You yelled at him in the middle of a restaurant. Which is part of why you were punished. But when you had a calm, thoughtful conversation with him about your feelings, he was more receptive."

I looked down at my feet. I guess I have been a bit more focused on the truth-telling part of the spell and not on how said truths were making other people feel. Mrs. Stevens probably thought the same thing. Gosh, I sounded like I was being a diva!

"Speaking of truths," Victoria said, "you still haven't told your dad about the play. You're running out of time, June!"

I felt my heart drop further into my chest. I'd made it through the entire winter break without telling him. "What are you going to say if he finds out?"

"How is he going to find out?"

"Um, perhaps from your mother?"

"I made her promise not to tell him!"

"You really want to make your mom an accessory to your lie?" Victoria said. "Listen, the sooner you tell him, the sooner he can react, and the sooner you all can have an honest conversation about your newfound interest in theater. Remember, I won't lift the spell unless you're completely—and respectfully—honest with him."

Victoria backed away from me and waved her magic wand above her head. A plume of dust and sprinkles started to spin around her, growing thicker and opaquer until I couldn't see her body anymore. Then the dust floated away, into thin air, leaving me standing alone on the sidewalk.

CONFESSION #107:

Nothing I do to get this spell lifted is right. I try to focus on telling the truth to everyone, and then I get in trouble for telling too much truth. But it's true that Carmen Evans forgot her dance steps and has two left feet. (I've seen her at birthday parties, the girl can't remember any of those TikTok dance challenges, so how is she going to remember *The Wiz* choreography?) And it's true Kevin Thomas forgot his lines. I mean Tinman only has a few lines anyway, how is it that he can't remember them? I don't believe he studied during Christmas break!

And Mrs. Stevens is a really tough director. She criticizes everything I do. Has she ever played Dorothy in *The Wiz*? I mean, I googled her and I couldn't find anything that she has starred in. She says she used to be in Broadway plays, maybe she meant off Broadway, like off off off off Broadway. Who knows if she's even a real actress? 🤔

And Victoria keeps changing the rules of the curse. Now it's "Tell the truth . . . but not too much"! How am I supposed to know exactly how much truth will get this gosh-darn spell lifted?

And then there's the whole issue of telling my dad, which I still haven't done. . . .

I know I have to live my truth—and I know now that acting is really what I want to do, even if I am bad at it! But I might have to sacrifice a few things—like the support of my father—in order to live my truth.

And I don't know if I'm ready for that yet.

CHAPTER FIFTEEN

Nia was still annoyed with me after the whole Lee thing had gone down. Since the beginning of the spring semester, she had stopped walking with Olive and me to school (she would walk with Olive to my house, then hurry ahead instead of waiting for me, and walk to school by herself. Super awkward). She hardly looked at me in class, but she always made a big effort to talk with Lee, especially at lunch. When he walked into class, she would greet him with "Hi, LEE! How ARE YOU?!" every time.

Lee gave me a polite "hi" every day, too, but Nia made sure to keep his attention so that he wouldn't have time to even think to ask me what was going on in my life. Had

Nia told him what I did (or didn't do)? Did he hate me for it?

Then, the day before yesterday, I heard Nia say, "Yesterday was fun! You should come over more often!" to Lee. So they *were* hanging out? Hanging out without me?

My heart fell into my shoes. I wrote a blog post:

CONFESSION #113:

I know they're hanging out. Without me. I'm sure they hang out and laugh and share hot chocolates and talk about me. I'm sure they think I'm the worst human in the world. I would kick it without me after what I did, too. But still, my Lee with *Nia*. Still doesn't seem right. It's not horrible. I would just prefer Lee hang out with me. I think. Is it possible to lose someone you never really had in the first place?

But as rehearsals continued, I paid less and less attention to Lee and Nia in class, because I was paying more attention to Alvin.

In science and English lit classes, Alvin had been sitting next to me instead of Lee since rehearsals had started. Maybe because we were both in the musical, we had more to talk about. Sometimes we talked about *The Wiz*. But sometimes we talked about music in general. Or singing. Or computer games. "You like *Mario Kart*?" he asked me once, and I said I did. "We should play sometime."

I hadn't played that game in a while, but after Alvin mentioned it, I remembered how much I liked it. Maybe I could find my old Nintendo Switch at my house somewhere and we could play together.

Together.

That thought made me all warm in my tummy. I thought about playing *Mario Kart* with Alvin through the rest of class that day. When the bell rang, I almost didn't notice Lee and Nia had walked out of class already, together.

✦

Lunch often made me feel nauseated. Not because I didn't like the mystery meat in the cafeteria (I didn't hate it, surprisingly), but because I never knew if Nia was going to be there or what her mood would be. When I was there, Nia barely sat at our table anymore. She often would get up to talk to other girls right as I sat down, or she would stay but then she wouldn't say anything to me at all. When she left the table, it felt like a sack of rocks settled in my stomach. It was pretty obvious to everyone that she was mad at me. Yesterday, I didn't even bother to come down to lunch altogether. Instead, I went to the library, getting some studying done and reading some articles about the history of the musical.

I sat alone at a corner table, out of sight from the head librarian, trying to concentrate on my math homework and sneak bites of my sandwich, though food wasn't really allowed in the library. My stomach cramped. I couldn't get comfortable in that hard wood chair, either. I felt . . . unsettled. Maybe it was because my friendship with Nia had frayed. Maybe it was because I didn't know if I was going to finish my homework in time. But my mind wandered to what Nia and Lee were talking about now. Were they talking about me? Did Lee know I'd avoided telling Nia how he felt? Did they both hate me?

I opened up my secret blog and started to write.

CONFESSION #115:

Fine, Nia, you do you. Throw away our friendship. Kick it with Lee. Have a blast. I won't think about you or him. No really. I don't need either one of you. I have my career! My CRAFT! That's something only fellow actors like Alvin would understand. . . .

"Working hard there?" I heard a familiar voice. Alvin was standing there with his tablet and a notebook. I quickly clicked out of my blog so he couldn't see the post and looked up at him, flustered.

"I figured I'd make this a working lunch," I replied.

"Word. Me too," he said. "Been working on some science homework." Alvin sat down in front of me.

"Where's Lee?" I asked.

"With Nia at our table. Olive had some orchestra thing, I think. I didn't want to be a third wheel. So I came here."

I smiled. Did he come to the library to work, or to look for me? I relaxed in my seat, enjoying my unexpected company. "So, how's life as a Scarecrow?" I said, trying to break the ice.

Alvin looked at me. "Well, I'm not sweating as much offstage without that crazy wig and old clothes."

I laughed. He certainly did look cool. Cool like, calm and collected. And like, cute. And, what was happening? What's up with my eyes—it seems like little fairy lights were dancing in front of me. Did I not have enough to eat for lunch?

"Anyway, you coming to rehearsals today? I think we're doing my Scarecrow number, so I'm not sure if you have to be there."

"I'll be there!" I said. "I pretty much come to every rehearsal."

"Yeah, I just didn't know because they're mostly my scenes and all. But yeah, come check it out. Let me know what you think."

I looked at him. Was he asking me to come watch because he wanted me to watch? "You want to know what *I* think of *you*? You're the professional! You sing all the time!"

Alvin clasped his hands together. "Yeah, but I want to know what you think. I mean, you are the star of the show."

I smiled, flattered at being called a star. "I'll be there."

"Great," he said. "I'll let you get back to your work. See you later."

With that, I tried to get back to my studies. I tried to think about anything other than Alvin looking at me and saying I was a star. But I failed immensely, and just sat there in my seat for another ten minutes, smiling, willing the day to whiz by fast so rehearsals could begin.

✦

I was walking from the library to my next class, my mind still racing about Alvin and *The Wiz* and homework and the annoying hole in my sock that was big enough for my big toe to poke through, which no one could see but I could feel.

I walked past the main office of the building, where the principal's office and the secretary's desk were. The school counselor's office was next to the main office, too, but I almost never saw anyone going in or out of it. But suddenly, the door opened. And, of all people, Nia stepped out in front of me, looking the opposite way.

"Whoa!" I said. My voice surprised her. She stopped moving.

Nia gasped. She looked like she'd seen a ghost, and like she was hoping the ghost didn't see her coming out of the school counselor's office. "You just running into people like that? DANG."

Was she trying to blame me for running into her? "You walked out the door and didn't see me," I said.

We locked eyes for a second, but it seemed like much longer. I saw Nia's cheeks turn redder and redder as we stood there. She looked guilty, like she'd been caught doing something she didn't want anyone to know she did. Like picking her nose or something. The school counselor's office. Why would she be in there? Was something going on?

"I gotta go," she finally said, then marched off. She didn't look back.

I watched her move quickly down the hallway—she didn't give any of her usual waves or nods.

I thought about Nia's attitude lately. Her negativity had reached an all-time high. Nia had her opinions on things, sure, but she used to find some humor in things she may not have liked as much as I did, or things we both didn't like at all. She would've cracked a few jokes or something. Lately, though, everything seemed boring or annoying to her. Or disappointing. Except for Lee.

Maybe there was something going on with Nia. Something she hadn't told me, which also would have been super weird. She told me everything! So I thought. This distance between us wasn't where I had seen our friendship going.

But it also explained a lot of why Nia and I had seemed so far apart lately.

CHAPTER SIXTEEN

Rehearsals were my escape from the drama in my life. I remembered what Mrs. Stevens said about my feedback to people. Maybe I had been a bit harsh. For example, the chorus dancers were good, though one of them almost poked Alvin in the eye once. But I didn't yell and scream at the girl. I didn't call out her mistake. I simply wrote it in my confessions.

CONFESSION #116:

Girl with the razor-sharp elbows and two left feet! Watch yourself! If you knock Scarecrow's eyes out, we're gonna have to rewrite the musical so Scarecrow begs for a brain AND an eye from the Wizard!

We started rehearsing the big dance numbers, which involved nearly all the cast members. Even I had trouble remembering every single dance move. But there were some kids who struggled more than others.

Take Jermaine Hill. When everyone went left, he went right. Every. Single. Time. I didn't say anything bad about him out loud, I typed my opinions in my blog:

Jermaine, this is how you find left. Stick two hands out in front of you. Hold your thumbs out, and your pointer fingers up. Whichever hand makes an

L shape, that's "left"! Didn't we learn this when we were in kindergarten?

And even after we put oil on Tinman, he still looked stiff while we danced to "Ease on Down the Road." But I said nothing. I just wrote it down in my secret blog.

Kevin dances like my great-grandfather (who's dead)—stiff, like a cardboard box.

And I know Stacey Blackstone was supposed to be Evillene, but I wasn't sure she was really . . . believable. Where was the edge? The side-eye? See, this is where Nia could have really shined had she considered auditioning. I took out my tablet again:

Nia would have made a great Wicked Witch of the West. Nia is a queen of side-eye and shade! The way that she's mad at me these days, she clearly has the anger. Maybe she can be a stand-in during one of our rehearsals.

I admit, not every performance of mine was perfect, either. I'd had my share of off notes or forgetting a line here or there. When I missed my cue during the Lion's big number, I caught it before anyone else did. "Darn it!" I said out loud. I felt that stabbing pain behind my eye. "It's okay, June, keep going," Mrs. Stevens encouraged. Maybe she didn't catch my mistake, but I did. But it also fueled me to hit my marks for the rest of the rehearsal.

HONEST June

CONFESSION #124:

This is where I belong. On the stage. Performing in front of an audience. Singing my little lungs out. Acting! This is different from other things I'm good at. I can study to be good at math. I can practice to be good at field hockey. But acting takes natural skill. It's like I'm myself, but better! I mean, I have to learn lines and practice dance moves, but it doesn't feel like work.

I feel like I'm really in my groove.

I could really be an actress.

After *The Wiz*, I should get an agent, like Ayanna

Pullman has. Maybe I should talk to her about life in Hollywood? I mean, she was an extra in that Fast and Furious movie last year. And then I could get a manager. And then my dad will see how serious I'm taking this acting thing and what a great advisement team I have around me. And then my career will take off, and then I'll be in movies, and get paid, and be able to buy things, and pay for my own college, and buy a few houses and my father wouldn't be able to say I didn't have a real career! In fact, maybe I could hire him to be my lawyer!

✦

The trickiest part of my schedule these days was managing *The Wiz* rehearsals with newspaper meetings. Rehearsals were every day, and newspaper meetings were Mondays, Wednesdays, and Thursdays. Ms. West was understanding about my conflict and assured me I could drop into newspaper meetings whenever I could to pitch stories. But I still wanted to be an active part of the paper, no matter how much I had going on with *The Wiz* and school. After all, I'd had a story on the front page of the paper last semester. I loved seeing my name on the front page, and

I wanted more front-page stories. But I hadn't written a great story since then. I didn't want people to forget me, or my solid news reporting abilities.

On Monday, I popped into the newspaper meeting, knowing that the day's rehearsals were going to be mainly for the orchestra and backup dancers. A few kids were typing away at computers and Ms. West was chatting with three other students. "So your stories will run next week," Ms. West told them. "Love the one about the eighth-grade knitting club."

"We have a knitting club?" I jumped in.

One of the girls turned toward me. "Yes, and it's nine members deep! We started it over winter break because we got knitting sets for Christmas. We've all made scarves together."

The girl held up a bulky multicolored piece of stretchy yarn that she had tucked under her arm. I raised my eyebrows and nodded, smiling politely. The three girls walked toward the computers, and I fished my phone out to type a quick blog post right there on the spot, before I blurted out something I would regret:

> This is newsworthy? Maybe they need a knitting advisor to help them make things people would actually wear.

"Hi, June," Ms. West said. "Nice to see you. How are rehearsals going?"

I quickly tucked my phone into my pocket. "They're great!" I said. "My first time acting, but I don't want it to be the last."

Ms. West nodded. "That's great. We'll probably do a story on opening night. I'm surprised you had time to come here. What's going on today?"

"I thought you'd need a story from me for the paper," I said. "You gotta have at least one hard-hitting journalist reporting on what's going on in the halls of FCMS."

Ms. West laughed. "Thanks, June. We have plenty of students contributing. In fact, we're all full up for the next issue. We're working on the issue coming out in three weeks."

I held my breath. So I hadn't been missed while I was away? Did Ms. West find someone else to do the front-page stories already? "Well, who is covering the news?"

"All of these kids!" Ms. West said. "We've got a profile on our football team for sports, we've got a story on the guest speaker coming next week during our all-school assembly, and we've got a piece on the new knitting club."

None of these stories sounded as interesting as mine. My hand was right on my phone, ready to write down what I really thought of these ideas so I didn't say how bored I was of them out loud. "Oh! I know!" I blurted out. "What about a profile of me, the lead actress in the play?"

Ms. West looked at me. Then she raised an eyebrow. "You're pitching a story about yourself for the paper?"

"Well, yes, I'm the lead actress! People want to know about me, right? It could be a profile on how I became an actress!"

Ms. West pursed her lips together and clasped her hands under her chin. "June, it's awesome you're the lead in the play. The week of the performances, we'll do a story on the production."

"Yeah, of course," I said. "But you could do one on me before that."

Ms. West clasped her hands tighter. "I think we'll just do the one big story on the cast. We're packed with stories leading up to that week anyway."

Ms. West walked toward the girls who'd pitched the story about the knitting club. I looked around the newsroom. Kids were busy going over notes and chatting excitedly about their stories. Ms. West gave one of them a high five. Was she not interested in my story idea? In my acting? But I was way more interesting than a knitting club! I was a field hockey–playing straight-A student who had never acted before and who had nailed the audition for the leading role in *The Wiz*! That was cover story material!

I sat down on the couch near the front of the newsroom and took out my phone. I felt a burning sensation in my belly, rising to my throat. I felt—gulp!—like I was no longer needed at the paper. Could that be possible?! I started to type before my mouth started talking.

CONFESSION #126:

Knitting club, seriously??? Knitting is the most boring thing ever! No one buys tickets to watch people knit! Famous knitters do not make the front page of newspapers. Or covers of magazines!

How am I not on the front page of the *Featherstone Post*? I am the lead actress in *The Wiz*! Surely all the teachers are talking about me, right? Breakout star? Does Ms. West know how hard I worked to get this role? How much studying goes into this role? Well, maybe I should pitch my story to a real news outlet. Like *People* magazine! Or *Variety*! Then I'd really get myself a top agent, like the one Ayanna Pullman has!

CHAPTER SEVENTEEN

Finally, after months of rehearsals, of singing in the shower, of practicing dance moves as I walked to school . . . it was showtime—opening night was tonight. And as much as I'd studied, rehearsed, sang, and watched YouTube clips of this musical, I still didn't feel ready. For one, I still didn't have the support of my best friend. Nia hadn't been returning any of my text messages or hanging out with me after school, partly because of basketball, but mostly because she was still upset with me after the Lee situation had gone down. And when I did get a response after sending twenty texts in a row . . .

JUNE: hello

JUNE: Hi

JUNE: Hey. 🤚

JUNE: You there?

JUNE: Nia?

JUNE: Nia!

JUNE: Girl, where are you?

JUNE: You still mad?

She responded with short answers.

NIA: Yes.

NIA: Girl, what?

NIA: No.

NIA: Nope.

NIA: Gotta go.

As soon as I woke up in the morning on the day of opening night, I sent one last text to her.

JUNE: Hey! You coming to opening night of the play? I'll see you there, right?!

NIA: No.

JUNE: What? You're my best friend!

I started to feel the nerves in my stomach.

NIA: Things are different now, June.

I took a breath, tired of fighting with her already.

JUNE: Different? Is this about Lee? C'mon, Lee will be there, too. Come and see us both! Okay, just come and see him. But please, come to the play.

She didn't respond.

So I put down my phone.

Besides Nia, I still hadn't yet told my dad I was starring in *The Wiz*. And I *knew* I had to. This was my last chance before the musical opened, and I didn't want Victoria to keep the spell on me forever, much less do something to embarrass me during my very first performance, like give me a sneezing fit or two left feet onstage. The universe had thrown me a bone—Dad had been pulling a lot of late nights at the office working on a big case, so he hadn't seen me come home late from rehearsal every day the past few months. But that had just given me an excuse to prolong the suspense. We were coming down to the final hours before the show. I had to tell him now, or never.

As I lay in bed I felt jittery and my anxiety was raging—no amount of deep breathing or meditation could calm me down right now. It felt like there was a Ping-Pong ball bouncing around in my insides. But I was hungry—I could have eaten anything that was hot and put on a plate in front of me. I had to go downstairs to breakfast, face my father, and confess the truth about the play. I steeled myself and swung my legs out of bed.

I dressed slowly and mindlessly, like I was swimming through water, and packed my backpack full of snacks, makeup, hair accessories, and everything else I could possibly need to get me through a full day of school and rehearsal, and straight to the play's opening notes at 7:00 p.m.

I stuck my head in the pantry looking for food just as my dad came downstairs to leave for work. "Hey, June, how's my baby girl doing?"

"Good," I said, grabbing a bowl of cornflakes and a banana and sitting down at our kitchen table. Mom walked into the kitchen quietly, observing our conversation.

"What's going on at school today?" he asked. This was my opening. I looked up at him. I had to find the words.

That familiar feeling of word vomit rose from my throat to my mouth and I knew there was no holding back. I wasn't even going to *try* to hold back this time. I instead looked at my dad and smiled, hoping the smile might make the truth sound a little better than it was, instead of it sounding like I was too scared to tell him months ago.

"I'm, um . . . I'm starring in the school musical today."

My dad looked at me blankly.

I cleared my throat and started again. "I'm starring in the school musical. The school is putting on a version of *The Wiz*, and I've been cast as Dorothy. And our first performance is tonight."

He stared at me, realization slowly dawning on his face. Then, suddenly, he looked as if I'd told him the biggest news to hit Featherstone Creek in decades. He sat down in a kitchen chair and held his chin thoughtfully. "You're the lead role? Why . . . what . . . that's great, June!"

This was not the reaction I expected. I was surprised. No anger? No "This is going to take time away from your studies"? No questioning about how I would support myself?

I gave a half smile. Dad leaned again toward me. "But how did I not know about this earlier?" *Because I made it my life's mission for the past few months not to tell you?* I thought to myself. I took a breath. The truth might even win me some sympathy from him. *Here goes. . . .*

"I didn't want to tell you because I didn't think you'd be supportive. You might see this as another distraction from school. So I was scared."

The caterpillar eyebrows scrunched together. Oh man, the telltale sign he was upset was when those eyebrows looked like caterpillars kissing. "June, you never have to be scared to tell me anything. I thought we went through this. I'm always going to be here for you."

"But you've always said that actors don't have real jobs."

Dad cleared his throat and looked at my mother. She raised an eyebrow. That was the look she gave him when someone had, in fact, told the truth and Dad could not wiggle his way out of the facts.

"Honey, this is acting in your school play. This is your very first time acting in anything. Why would I put all that kind of pressure on you, to expect that you would make a career out of it?"

I looked at him. "What if I do want to make a career out of it, Dad? I really like acting! I really like how I feel when I'm acting."

My dad sat at the table and looked between my mom and me. "Did you know about this?" he asked her.

"She told me a while back, and I promised to let her tell you herself," Mom said.

Dad looked frustrated. "I'm upset that I'm the last person to know about this. I would have wanted to celebrate! When exactly did you get the news, June?"

My nose prickled. I cleared my throat. "The audition was the Monday after Thanksgiving break."

Dad pretended to smack his hand against his forehead. "I could have been bragging to my friends since November that my baby was going to be Dorothy in the school play?!"

He stood up from the table and looked for his phone. "If my baby girl is going to play Dorothy in *The Wiz*, then I want to be there. The whole *town* should be there. Will the whole town be there? I should invite my entire firm. Where can I buy tickets?"

The entire town? *Would* the entire town be there? Mom's family? Uncle Ray? Nia's family?

I looked at him and blinked quickly in response. I suddenly felt intensely queasy, and hoped my cornflakes stayed in my belly. I could imagine seeing Dad from the stage—I'd pictured it for months. But I had purposely blocked from my head the vision of hundreds of people sitting in the seats judging my performance so I didn't get stage fright. But now I felt it. I had a headache. My stomach tightened. And then, more word vomit came out. "Maybe you shouldn't come," I said in a panic, and immediately sucked in my breath.

Did I just disinvite my own *father* to the school musical?!

"Maybe you shouldn't come, uh, because it's, like, it's my first performance and you know I'm nervous enough already," I stammered. "I just don't want to disappoint you."

He backed away from me, the eyebrows drawing closer together on his forehead. "Are you saying you don't want me there?"

"No, I'm just saying, like, I don't know. . . ." My stomach got even queasier. My dad looked disappointed, more disappointed than when I told him that I didn't want to go to Howard. The anxiety over opening night, over my performance, over the audience, over my dad—every bad feeling swelled up in my stomach all at once. And I couldn't breathe.

Dad looked at me, confused. I couldn't stomach my fear and this uncomfortable conversation one second longer. I was making things messier with every word. I felt like I'd been hit by a bus—anxious about performing, nervous about telling Dad the truth, and the cornflakes wanted to hurl themselves from my belly, so I got up from the table and ran into the washroom before they could, and I sat on the floor of the bathroom, alone, wishing I could click my heels like Dorothy does in the musical and instantly be back in my bedroom, safely under the covers.

As I sat there grabbing my knees, trying to get my stomach to feel a little better, I noticed a small sprinkle of dust in the air. It grew to a larger sprinkle of dust, and then a tall body of dust. Victoria had squeezed her way into this half bathroom. Privacy was just not a virtue of this spell.

"Are you happy now?" I asked. "Told my dad the whole thing." I felt tears pricking at my eyes. I'd been awake for maybe thirty minutes and I was already exhausted. I wanted to crawl back into bed and hide under the covers. I wanted this day to be over already.

"I can see that," Victoria said. She crouched down by me and took my hands in hers. "I also think nerves have gotten the best of you, honey."

"I'm only about to give the most important performance of my life in front of my father and mother and the entire town! Except for my best friend because she wants nothing to do with me!" I wailed, and hiccuped.

Victoria sat down next to me. "Take one breath at a time, and think about one minute at a time. The only thing you must do right now is go out there and tell your dad you want him to come to the show tonight. Start there."

"And then what?"

"And then go to school, and don't think any more about that musical until you step on that stage. You've prepared, and you have rehearsed. You're going to make a wonderful Dorothy. That's it!"

"Are you sure?" I asked, wiping at my tears and sniffling.

"I'm positive of it. Now, go back outside and re-invite your father to the show."

Victoria disappeared in a poof. I gathered my wits about me. I took a few deep breaths and stood up. I looked at myself in the mirror. *I memorized my lines. I've rehearsed. I'm ready.*

I opened the bathroom door and I walked out ready to properly invite my dad to the show. I took another deep breath and walked into the kitchen. I looked around. No dad, no briefcase. He was already gone.

Mom looked over at me and put her hands on my shoulders. I felt even more worried. "I just made it all worse. He might not even come!"

"He'll be there," Mom said. "Meanwhile, it's late. I saw Nia and Olive walk by already."

"Nia doesn't want to see me. She's already told me she's not coming tonight."

"Really?" Mom said with eyebrows raised.

"I've made a mess of everything," I admitted, and hung my head.

Mom squeezed my shoulders. "C'mon, baby, I'll give you a ride to school."

We drove to school quickly—my mother was already wearing her scrubs and was planning to head to the hospital for a delivery right afterward. "Cheer up, honey, tonight is your big night!"

"But my people won't be there to support me. No Dad, no Nia. . . ."

Mom pulled into the circular drive in front of school and put the car in park. I unbuckled my seat belt so I could jump out. "First, Nia. What's going on there? You guys drifting apart or something?"

"No!" I exclaimed. "Nia's my very best friend."

"Have you told her that lately?" Mom asked, and pursed her lips. "Have you explained how much she really means to you? That you two are practically sisters? That she's been there for you for every big moment in your life?"

I thought for a moment. “I guess I assumed she knew.”

“Why don’t you tell her? Write her a note of appreciation. Tell her you can’t be Dorothy without her support.”

Mom stroked my cheek with her hand and gave me a kiss on the forehead. “We’ll be here for the start of the show, I promise.”

“We?” I asked hopefully.

“Yes, your dad and I. I’ll get him there, don’t worry. Remember, think of yourself on that stage, having fun with your friends, doing what you love. You got this!”

I gave my mom a smile and got out of the car. I pulled my backpack over my shoulder, took a deep breath, and walked toward the door with my head held high. *Maybe she’s right,* I thought. *I mean, she has played Dorothy before.* She’d know a Dorothy when she saw one.

CHAPTER EIGHTEEN

I stood backstage, shivering like I'd just eaten a slushie, and peeked through the curtain to look out at the crowd. I felt my hands get clammy and I fidgeted in my shoes, rocking back and forth as I held on to the curtain. Parents and kids were starting to take their seats, chatting and greeting each other as they filled the auditorium. This was it. My acting debut.

I'd texted Nia once more that afternoon during our dress rehearsal to see if she would be there tonight. I hadn't heard back. I'd also asked Mom again if she thought Dad would be there, and she hadn't gotten back to me, either. She simply texted back, "Good luck!"

Then my phone vibrated one more time:

CHLOE: Break a leg! GOOD LUCK, DOROTHY!

I needed that note of encouragement. I stopped fidgeting for a few moments.

"June, wardrobe!" Mrs. Stevens called for me. I shut the curtain and turned back toward the right side of the backstage area, where the costumes were hanging. I had my hair pulled back behind a headband, with two high bunches that were round and full, similar to Diana Ross's short Afro in the movie. My costume, a pale lavender dress, was pretty and moved with me for every turn. "Look at you," Mrs. Stevens said. "Looking like a real Dorothy."

I looked over and saw a kid wearing oversized shoes and baggy brown shorts. Patches of straw trailed him when he walked over. "How do I look?" Alvin said.

"OMG, I didn't recognize you," I said. "You look . . . kinda itchy. But amazing!"

"You look great," Alvin said. "This costume is a bit warm, though. Hope I don't slip on my own sweat."

Inside, I swooned. Alvin thought I looked great! I hoped I would perform as good as I apparently looked. I glanced around at the entire production. Kids were dressed up like Munchkins or various animals. The Tinman walked

by stiffly, wrapped in aluminum foil and wearing a silver pyramid-shaped hat. I even saw Lee dashing out from behind the scenes, helping put the finishing touches on parts of the background scrim. It felt like marbles were rolling around in my stomach. I was going to be onstage in less than ten minutes!

I looked for my book bag and reached for my phone again. I texted Nia.

JUNE: Girl, are you coming tonight?

Still no answer.

My stomach continued to flip-flop. I was now pacing around the backstage area, trying to get out some of the preshow jitters. Mrs. Stevens caught me talking to myself. "You okay, June?"

"Yeah, fine," I said. Then I felt a sneeze coming on. *Achoo!*

Mrs. Stevens put a hand on my shoulder. "Relax, June. You got this. Deep breaths."

I took a big inhale in, and let the air slowly seep out of my mouth. I tried to think about other things: the weather, key lime pie. And then a vision came to my head—I remembered the time during Christmas break when Alvin and I danced around my living room rehearsing, no one watching us, no Mrs. Stevens, no parents. I smiled to myself. I looked at Alvin across the backstage area. He gave me another thumbs-up.

I peeked outside through the curtains one last time to see if I could see anyone of note. And then I held my breath. There, in the front row, was my dad, sitting next to my mom. I smiled big and wide, thrilled that he had made it. I scanned the crowd in the rows behind him, wondering if I could recognize any other faces. Three rows above my parents, I saw Kevin Thomas's mom and dad sitting together. I still didn't see Nia. But the show had to go on.

At least my mom *and* my dad were there to support

me. I started to relax in my shoes, and the house lights flashed once, then twice. I took a deep breath, and the music began. It was time to hit the stage.

✦

I barely remember what happened during the first half of the musical—it felt like a blur. I know I danced and sang and I knew my lines and recited them just like I'd rehearsed. But I don't remember feeling anxious when I was onstage. Instead, it felt like I had drifted to another world, like I had transformed into another person.

I kind of felt like Victoria probably does—after all, she's this ghostlike creature that transforms into a human and walks among us when she needs to flex her superpower. I was doing the very same thing—flexing my superpower to transform into an actress.

Time seemed to have stood still but also pass by in a flash, so I couldn't believe it when I hit my last line of the first act. The cast shuffled backstage as the house lights came up and the crowd applauded. Intermission.

My heart was racing. I looked around and got caught up in the rush of the production—the change of set, the change of costume for the dancers before act two. Students were whizzing by to get to their next mark, or change clothes, or grab a sip of water before the curtain went back up.

A few minutes later, the house lights started to fade again, a signal to everyone to take their seats again as the show was about to restart. I took my place in the wings and got ready for our next number, the opening of act two. I took a peek from behind the curtain to check the audience once more. The music began and the curtain drew upward. Showtime.

We greeted the huge fire-breathing head Wizard, killed Evillene, and performed our big dance numbers to celebrate a brand-new day. We met the true wizard and discovered the heart for the Tinman and a brain for the

Scarecrow were within them all along. I clicked my heels and I brought myself back home. And like that, the curtain dropped and the show was over. The thunderous applause filled the auditorium. I could hear every sound in the seats—my mom calling out my name, Mr. Thomas's enthusiastic clapping. The curtain raised up again and the house lights turned on, so I could see the other students smiling at their parents. This felt like graduation—the joy, the hope, the pride—but it was a celebration of singing and dancing. My body had a wonderful tingly feeling, like excitement and happiness and clouds and sparkles and cotton candy all wrapped up around me. I'd done it—I'd gotten through the performance, and I'd loved every second of it!

"All right, back to the stage to take your bow!" Mrs. Stevens shouted to the cast.

The cast and crew rushed onstage and grabbed each other's hands to bow. I looked around and took in the cheers and the happy faces of the rest of the cast. I spotted Alvin in the group—he gave me a thumbs-up and grabbed my hand to take our separate bow as the leads.

"Wooo-*hooo*!" the crowd bellowed. I heard a recognizable holler from the front row, a man in a suit alternating pumping his fists in the air and clapping. My dad was screaming over most of the crowd and pointing at me. "That's my girl!" he said. "That's my girl!" Mom stood next to him, her smile as big as her face. She gave me a wink.

I hadn't felt this type of joy in a long time, not even after winning our last field hockey match. We came off the stage cheering and high-fiving, excited and proud. Mrs. Stevens gathered us over to one side. "That was excellent!" she declared. "I'm so proud of all of you. All that hard work during rehearsals really paid off. I could not have asked for a better performance." We all cheered and nodded at each other. "Now go out and get your mamas and daddies and let's celebrate opening night!"

CHAPTER NINETEEN

I removed my costume and stage makeup and came out from backstage and into the lobby of the school auditorium, immediately spotting my parents. My dad was beaming proudly, talking with the family standing next to him. He saw me midconversation and stuck out both of his arms to greet me.

"You were wonderful!" Mom said, hugging me. I buried my head into her chest and was enveloped in warmth. "My baby out there acting like Diana Ross. Like she's been doing this all her life! Maybe we should get you an agent!"

"I agree!" Dad said. "I still can't believe you didn't think I'd support you in this. You belong on the stage!"

I looked at my dad. "Does that mean I don't have to go out and get a real job?"

"Well, no, but I should stop saying that acting isn't a real job. Anything can be a real job if you excel at it and get paid for your skills. And if you want to pursue acting, of course I would support you. June, you were a star up there."

I couldn't believe what I was hearing. My dad, the lawyer, encouraging me to pursue the unpredictable career of an actress. Had my performance convinced him I had a real shot as an actress? Maybe *The Wiz* had stoked some creative fire in him? Could I move to Hollywood?

Just then, Blake and Olive came up beside me. "Whew! We did it!"

"You were awesome, June," Blake said. The three of us gave each other a group hug.

"Thanks, Blake! I saw you dance by me in the 'Brand New Day' scene! You were great, too! And, Olive, the orchestra was fantastic! How did you learn those songs so fast?"

"Practiced, just like you did."

"Right, duh!"

"We should celebrate all of our hard work," Olive said.

"Yes! Sleepover? My place? After the final show?" I offered. My parents nodded, and Blake and Olive smiled in agreement.

I still hadn't seen Nia, and at this point had to accept that she never came. "Have you seen Nia? Or heard from her?"

"No," Olive said. My heart sank. "I'm sure she just got caught up in something," Olive said. "Text her what's up when you get home."

"Right," I said. I looked around. I recognized a lot of parents as I scanned the crowd. Carmen's parents congratulated Carmen and chatted with Kevin's parents. I saw Alvin's parents next to Mrs. Stevens. And I saw Lee's grandparents, who had found my parents in the crowd and come over to say hello.

"Hey." I heard a familiar voice from behind me.

"Lee!" I said. "We did it, huh?"

"Yeah," he said. "I'm happy the Oz Forest stayed standing during the whole play."

"The set looked awesome," I said.

"Thanks. You were a great Dorothy."

"You think?"

"Yeah, really good." He laughed awkwardly. We both stood in front of each other and shuffled our feet, not sure what to say next.

"You seen Nia?" he asked.

"Nope," I said. "Not in a while." Which, unfortunately, was true.

"Oh," he said. "Was hoping we would all go out afterward. But that's okay. Maybe we can hang out Sunday after the last performance? Maybe go to the park if the weather isn't bad?"

Even though I was crazy jealous about Lee having an interest in Nia earlier, I missed them both. Between the fight, and studying for the play, I hadn't had a good hang with all my friends since Christmas. "Yeah, cool, Lee. And if it's too cold, we can all hang at my house."

"Cool," Lee said. "All right, I'm going to chat with my granny and gramps. I'll see you." I watched him walk off and smiled. In fact, I *just* smiled. I didn't blush, or get flustered, or have that weird glittery feeling in my belly like I had in the past. Was this because I knew he had a thing for Nia? Was this because I didn't have enough bandwidth in my brain for a crush *and* an utter obsession with my newfound creative work? Maybe I already had the glittery feeling inside me . . . except it was just joy over the musical instead of a crush on a boy.

As Lee made his way toward his grandparents, I saw Alvin talking with his parents and Mrs. Stevens. He caught my eye and gave me a nod, then dashed behind the adults, so I lost track of him for a moment. I saw him reappear with a bunch of the fake sunflowers from the forest set and walk toward me. "For you, Dorothy," he said.

"Oh my gosh, Alvin!"

"What, they're for congratulations! No big deal."

I felt like they were a big deal. A nice gesture from Scarecrow. "Thank you, Alvin," I said, smiling. "What's next, the school talent show or something?"

"I dunno," Alvin said. "Probably keep singing in church. Maybe I'll write a song. Or just go back to humming under my breath as I code."

I shifted from one leg to another. "Let me know if you ever want to watch *The Wiz* again for fun," I said shyly, and blushed.

Did I smile like this with Lee?

"Okay," Alvin said, also blushing.

Just then, Lee came back over to give Alvin a fist bump. "Nice work, bruh," he said. "Told you my man was like a regular Leon Bridges."

"Right," I said. "He certainly is."

Lee looked at me, unsure if he should stay. Alvin smiled and looked down at his shoes, and I didn't know where to look, so I kept looking at the flowers he'd brought me. Lee looked at them, too. We all smiled to ourselves.

Omg . . . omg . . . ! I did it! I was Dorothy, onstage, in front of the entire school. The entire town, even! And it felt great! I didn't fumble my lines. I felt so happy onstage. And all eyes were on me, singing along, dancing, having fun, everyone being entertained by my every move. I was, as the great Oscar-winning actors of our time have said, "giving the people what they wanted"! My dad was so impressed, he said I could be an actress in the future if I wanted. Could this be my new calling? Is it time to get an agent??? Maybe I should ask Ayanna who her agent is . . . would that be weird?

Mrs. Stevens was impressed with me, too. Which is amazing considering nothing really impresses her (except the color black, it seems, since she only wears black). I mean, I did carry the play—you know, because everyone was staring at me the whole time. And I noticed that Carmen messed up the dance steps like usual, but that's okay. She's not that great a dancer anyway, so people probably weren't paying her any attention. And Kevin was okay as Tinman—he was supposed act stiff anyway. 🤷🏾‍♀️

I wonder when they'll announce another play. I followed my true passion, and now I might become an actress. I told the truth and my family and friends were still there to support me. Lee even wanted to hang out with Nia and I said yes, because I know I shouldn't keep my two friends apart if they really like each other.

SO . . . if I've lived my truth, told my friends about their crushes on each other, and told my dad about the musical, shouldn't that be enough to get me out of this gosh-blessed spell? Victoria's got to let me go now, right? 😇

CHAPTER TWENTY

We performed *The Wiz* two more times over the weekend, closing our run of the musical Sunday afternoon. And in the crowd on Sunday, just before the start of the second act, I saw someone I hadn't expected would show—Nia.

I felt a wave of relief. Hopeful, even. Maybe this meant she wasn't mad at me? Maybe she wanted to support me after all? I rocked the last half of the show, even lighter on my feet than I had been for the previous performances. But when we took our final bows, I looked toward where Nia was sitting earlier. She was already gone.

I spent Sunday night celebrating our performances with Blake, Olive, Alvin, and Lee, and though I was a little disappointed Nia wasn't there to hang out with us, the night was still super fun. When all of it was over, I slept more soundly than I had in weeks. I felt like a weight had been lifted off my shoulders, and the buzzing high I felt from performing had eased up only slightly. I was still beaming from my acting accomplishments. And already thinking about my next big role.

I woke up with the sun on Monday, flung the covers off my body, and hopped out of bed, excited to face the day. School was closed for a teachers' development day, so there was only one day until I'd get to face my friends and teachers and peers, ready to receive the good vibes I earned from my play performance. Maybe I could finally get that profile in the school newspaper I pitched to Ms. West! She would be assigning my profile for the school newspaper after my showstopping performances, right? I went to the bathroom to get ready for the day, brushing my teeth, still humming "Ease on Down the Road" under my breath.

I returned to my room and heard my phone vibrate. It kept vibrating, like I had several texts or emails or notifications coming in at once. Except . . . the vibrating didn't stop. I went to pick up my phone and realized I had thirty notifications. *Wow, the rave reviews of my performances must be in,* I thought to myself. Olive had left ten of the thirty notifications:

OLIVE: Girl.

OLIVE: Seriously, girl. wake up

OLIVE: Have you seen this? Did you really? Girl. I mean. How could you?

What was she talking about? I texted her back.

JUNE: What do you mean?

JUNE: What did I do? Go to sleep without texting you?

OLIVE: Girl. Check. Your. Email.

I closed the text messages and hopped on my computer, pulling up my email inbox.

I had nearly fifty unread messages, the most emails I'd

ever had in one day. Some names I recognized, but others were new. New fans, perhaps?

Then I read some of the subject headlines. "Girl, really?" "You're the worst." "How dare you." "Two-faced." "Mean Girl."

What were people talking about? All of this from my performance? I clicked open one of the emails. A link to my blog had been posted at the bottom. I did a double take. I opened another one, and the same link was posted within that email, too. OMG. People knew about my blog? My secret online diary? How did these people find out? Oh my bleezus, had some hacker found my secret

blog and sent it to all of Featherstone Creek?! I mean, they couldn't even get into it—it was password protected. I had a very secret, very hard-to-crack password on it! That no one knew! Right? *Right?! RIGHT??!?!!!!?!?*

I opened another email, which also had the same link posted. This time I clicked on the link to my blog, just to make sure that it was still private. *It better still be private,* I thought to myself, *because if it's not, it would . . . be . . . ah . . .*

The link went directly to my blog. My entire blog. Every post, every confession, accessible. There was no sign-in page, no log-in. *Is. This. Really. Happening?* It felt like the blood stopped pumping to my brain. Like I might just drop into my shoes and get sucked into the center of the earth. Was my blog now public? How in the world did this get released to the public? Could everyone see it now?

Could. Everyone. SEE IT. *Now?*

I texted Olive.

JUNE: Are you talking about Honest June?

OLIVE: You mean Two-Faced June? The June who has a private blog

where she writes mean things about people? That June who has an online burn book?

I'm dead.

"How . . . in the world . . . did you get into my private blog?" I whispered. I could barely get out the words because I was one hundred percent actually deceased.

OLIVE: Well, it's not private anymore, June. You sent an Instagram out to the entire town publicizing it!

I felt like all the oxygen had been sucked out of the room. "What are you talking about?!" I yelled out loud. I pulled up Instagram on my phone. I looked at my feed, and the most recent post was a photo of myself in my room, with a caption that read, "Come check out my new unfiltered blog! It's full of the real tea on everyone at Featherstone Creek!" The caption included a direct link to my blog.

What. In. All. That. Is. REAL? Why the heck would I publicize my own secret blog???

There was no way I could have posted the photo. In fact, it was impossible for me to have done it, because according to the time stamp, it had been posted eighteen hours ago—when I was onstage during the school play! Someone had gotten into my Instagram account and created the post to make it look like I shared the blog myself.

Which meant, based on some of the unfiltered truths I had written in my blog . . . someone was trying to make me the most hated person in all of Featherstone Creek.

I clicked back to my inbox and started reading through the emails. I clicked open the one titled "Really?!?!" and saw they had linked to the entry about me admitting I didn't like Carmen's dancing. I opened another email, from Olive. She included a link to the blog post where I admitted Mrs. Charles's voice sounded like nails grating against a chalkboard to me, like when she says the word "bag" but it sounds more like "beeg." The blog posts about Lee, about Nia, about my parents, about teachers, classmates, people in town, were all *public.* Every nasty thing I had ever written, ever since Victoria landed me with this cursed truth-telling spell.

I slunk down in my desk chair and grabbed the sides

of my desk. I felt woozy. I thought I'd fall clean out of my chair.

All my unfiltered truths that I'd specifically written down in this very super-private, password-protected place so no one would ever see them had now been exposed.

I wanted to melt into a puddle. Could I shape-shift like Victoria? Maybe Victoria would turn me into fairy dust when she showed up to comment on this disaster? Yeah, and then I could disappear into the ether and not worry about all of Featherstone Creek wanting to see me plastered with eggs or tarred and feathered or otherwise punished for talking trash about everyone behind their back. Anything would be better than living on this earth after my secret blog had been hacked.

How could this have happened?

I called Olive immediately. She picked up the phone with a curt, "Girl."

I didn't have an explanation. I was silent, still like a statue.

"Did you really write all of this?" she said.

I have to say something. "I mean . . . it's a private diary. No one was supposed to see it! Who leaked my private blog?"

Olive let out a few noises that sounded like anger, disbelief, and distrust all at once. "It might be a private diary, but this is what you really think about people? Your best friends? About me? You said you think I let people walk all over me—is that true?"

I gulped. I couldn't find the words to explain myself.

"You talked about all of our friends at school here. Our parents. . . . You go around pretending you like everyone and then you talk about them behind their back?"

I couldn't feel my lips. My heart was beating at twice the normal rate.

"Do you think no one is perfect except for you?"

I wanted to disappear into the walls.

"This is, like, the lowest thing I've ever seen somebody do. Like, this hurts."

"I'm sorry, I was . . . I didn't mean what I said about you. I don't think you're a pushover. . . ."

"That's not what your blog says," she countered. Then Olive hung up on me.

I closed my eyes and hung my head. I never wanted to hurt any of my friends, but I would especially never want to hurt Olive. She's unbelievably kind; she couldn't hurt a mosquito.

A thought struck me like lightning. I *had* to call Nia. If there was one person I dunked on the most on the blog, it was Nia. I called her petty, mean, cruel. I took all my frustrations about our friendship falling apart out on this blog, with the intention that she would never see it. But she had by this point, obviously. And at this moment—she'd have to hate me. I would hate me, too. I texted her. Twelve times. I got no response.

I flung myself back on the bed. I looked at the emails. Some of my field hockey teammates had responded to the post I made about Kenya not being able to defend the team from a sack of potatoes, or Coach Dwight favoring me over Natalie Cross for a starting position because Natalie is slower than molasses left out in the cold. One person sent me a whole email's worth of sobbing emojis, another an email full of steam-headed angry emojis. Guess I wouldn't be rejoining the team now—how could I play on a team full of girls who hated me?

I closed my eyes and prayed that my bed could somehow become a pool of water or dust cloud of some sort and scoop me up to take me to the next realm. Just wash me away. Far, far away.

Just when I thought this was the worst that I could feel, I started to cough. I felt dust in the air. My coughing got stronger and stronger, like a thick trail of chimney smoke surrounded me. I knew what was happening. *Who,* rather, was happening. Victoria. Perfect timing.

She said nothing when she came into view. I said nothing in return. Instead, tears started to stream down my face. I couldn't keep it in anymore. I felt sorry I had said all those nasty things—but I felt especially sorry that this was all happening to me.

"Well, this is a real pickle, huh?" Victoria said, her eyebrows knotted together. "I wanted you to learn your lesson, but I didn't want you to hurt a bunch of people in the process."

I looked up at her, suddenly flush with rage. "Learn my lesson?!"

"June, I told you, I watched your every move. I knew you had a secret blog where you were saying things you didn't want other people to know and using it to get around the restrictions of the spell," she said.

I knew it. She wanted this to happen! She could have stopped me from writing my truths down, but instead she wanted me to get burned. She burned me. She . . . unleashed the blog on purpose.

"This is all your fault!" I yelled. "The truth-telling, the blog, the everything. It's all your fault. If I didn't have this spell problem, this would have never happened! You're the one who made the blog public!"

"June, this is not *my* fault. I didn't tell you to create a blog where you'd trash-talk people behind their backs. And I'm certainly not the one who made that post on your Instagram about it."

"*You* said I had to tell the truth no matter what! I couldn't say half the things that I thought out loud—people would have never spoken to me again! This stupid blog was my only option! It was supposed to be safe—from *you*!"

Victoria moved to stand directly in front of me, crossing her arms. "This spell was supposed to help you tell all truths—the good, the helpful, as well as the not-so-good ones. June, let's be honest—your blog reads like the Daily Featherstone Creek Nastygram. You can't write in a diary that people's acting sucks and then smile in their faces the next day. June, listen, honey—of course it matters *if* you tell the truth—but even more so, it matters *how* you tell

the truth! And writing all of your mean feelings in a secret blog is not the way to deal with them!"

The tears fell from my face, making the front of my shirt wet. I realized I had hurt people with my words, the exact opposite of what I wanted to do. I had never intended to hurt anyone! That's why I held in my truths for so long. I did everything I could to get the spell lifted; I'd been so focused on telling the truth that I didn't care how it came out. And now I felt the same way people probably felt when they saw my horrible opinions of them on the blog. Heartbroken. Betrayed. Sitting alone crying heavy, uncontrollable tears that choked my breathing and left me gasping for air, for peace. For someone's help.

I thought about all the things I said in the blog, and wiped at my face with the back of my hand. The complaints about my mom's food. My dad's lack of interest in culture. Me admitting I clogged the toilet on the first day of school. Me saying Olive's version of "Single Ladies" on the viola was corny. (I still thought she was super talented, because I can't play that song on any instrument. Not even a paint bucket!). I insulted teachers, our principal. Lee's parents, for leaving him behind. I said the famed hot dogs at Van's tasted like leather. Van's son was in the seventh grade. What if no one went to Van's anymore and the restaurant had no customers and stopped making money and went out of business because I said I didn't like the hot dogs? What if Van had to move and his son couldn't go to school anymore and they became homeless, all because of me? Because of Victoria's spell!

Wait.

I'd also written about Victoria in the blog posts.

I wrote about being put under the spell by Victoria. How was it that no one was talking about Victoria? Or the spell?

"I wrote about you on the blog, too. So now everyone's going to know about you and what you did to me. That will get me out of this, right? People will feel bad for me and forgive me for acting the way I did!"

Victoria looked at me. "Actually, no. No one knows about me."

I shook my head. "How is that possible?"

"See, when you're a fairy godmother, you have special powers. And another one of my great special powers is that when people write about me or try to reveal things about me in public, I can erase them."

Are you kidding me?

"So, what, you deleted yourself from my blog?"

Victoria put her hands to her collarbone, like she was clutching her pearls. "I had to. If I go public, I'd lose my fairy godmother accreditation. It's like losing your passport—you can't get back into Fairy Godmother world unless you stay secret."

So she put me in this situation and then left me out in the world with no defense when I got myself into real trouble? She was supposed to be my ally! She supposedly put me under this spell to help me "live my best life." I closed my eyes and rolled my eyeballs back into my skull.

"This whole thing is all your fault," I spat.

"No, dear," Victoria said. "I gave you a very special tool to help you learn how to be honest with people. You could have used that gift to help you let go of thinking you had to say the right things to make people happy, and learn that people can handle your opinions—when you give them in a thoughtful way—without getting mad at you or feeling bad about themselves. Instead, you didn't tell people how you felt to their face and wrote down your thoughts in a burn book."

I slid down the side of my bed and crumpled into a heap on the floor. Tears welled up in my eyes again and I tucked myself into a ball. I wondered if I could make like Rip Van Winkle and sleep for one hundred years and wake up when this nightmare was over.

Then, I felt a hand on my shoulder.

"Listen, June, honey. I know this situation sucks. However," Victoria said, "I *can* help you get out of this."

CHAPTER TWENTY-ONE

"It's all over," I said.

"What, the musical?" Chloe said on FaceTime an hour later. We hadn't spoken since opening night, but this time I'd called her not to discuss my fabulous acting debut, but rather my horrible personal situation.

"No," I said. "My life. My life is over."

"What happened now?" Chloe asked. "Your dad won't let you act anymore?"

"I almost wish that were my problem," I said, and sighed heavily. "My secret blog got exposed."

Chloe took a beat. "Ooooh," she said. "Exposed where?"

"To the entire internet-connected world."

Chloe looked more surprised than shocked. "Then why didn't I see it?"

"Girl, you don't know? No one sent you a link? Seems the entire universe got an email alert to this thing."

I sent Chloe a link so she could see what I was talking about. She was quiet for a minute as she clicked through her emails and then onto the blog. Then she realized just how bad this was. "Girl. *Girl!* Oooooh, June . . . ," she said.

"I know," I said.

"Dang, you really went in on Nia, huh?"

Nia was the one who got the brunt of my opinions, and I'd realized this. Anyone reading the blog would wonder why we were friends at all. "I didn't want to hurt people's feelings so . . ."

"So talking behind people's backs was better?" Chloe continued.

I was getting my due punishment, no doubt about it, and justly. The whole school probably hated me. My parents would think I was horrible when they found out. (Thank God they weren't big social media users. . . .) Victoria wouldn't lift the spell. I'd managed to burn my entire reputation with this blog.

Chloe read while she sat on FaceTime with me. She laughed. "Why are you hating on your math teacher so much?"

"All right, you can stop reading, geez!"

"What are you going to do?"

"Move in with you in California."

“Running from your problems won’t help. Besides, that Victoria can appear anywhere. She’d just follow you.”

She was right about that. I was running out of options. And allies. I had offended just about everyone at school with that blog and I’d have to face them all eventually. But for now, I didn’t want to face anyone. Not even my family. Not even myself.

✦

I didn’t leave my room all day. Mom was at the hospital, and after breakfast, Dad did yardwork for the whole day—he’d taken the day off so he could be home while I wasn’t in school. Luisa knocked on my door a few times, concerned, but I told her I didn’t need anything. I couldn’t get out from under my bedsheets. I was still hoping the sheets would swallow me alive and take me to another world where I didn’t have to face anyone from Featherstone Creek ever again.

My life at FCMS was over. No point in trying to show my face again. No one would care to see me. I had no friends, no social life, no future. Goodbye, Featherstone Creek. I should've started looking at other places to live. To start over. Like . . . Hollywood? Might as well get that acting career started now. I could change my name to a stage name in the process, and really give myself a fresh start.

I looked in my closet for my suitcases. I wondered how much of my stuff I could pack with me as I left town. I'd probably have to hitch a ride with a trucker or someone with pity and space in the back seat. If I was going to be hitchhiking, I shouldn't pack too much. Who knows how far I'd have to hike before I found a ride, plus I couldn't crowd up a stranger's car with all my luggage.

Luggage. Packing. *Oh no.*

The school camping trip.

The spring camping trip, where the school took over an entire campground on Lake Lanier and arranged cook-outs and activities and games and a sleepover for all the students, was coming up in a few weeks. I'd completely forgotten in all the musical madness. It was the epic kick-off to spring break. And everyone usually went. Students would be staying a long weekend with a select group of parents and teachers as chaperones. At a campground with plenty of dark woods, and rivers, and caves, and wild animals. . . .

How was I supposed to travel to the woods with people

who clearly now hated me? I couldn't imagine worse punishment. I would have to be sitting in the woods with the same people I had insulted in my blog. Wouldn't they just want to get their revenge on me? Maybe they'd put bedbugs in my sleeping bag, or leave me out in the woods, exposed to the elements. That's it—that was how I would end up leaving this world, hearing my own words being used against me, with my friends quoting my mean blogs back to me.

My truth would end up killing me.

My chest felt so tight that breathing felt like sandpaper was rubbing my insides. I had a headache. The doom of the situation hung on my body like a heavy cape. I couldn't see a way out. I turned toward my bed and flopped down face-first into a pillow.

I heard a knock on the door. "June?" my dad called out.

Oh man. He opened the door and walked toward my bed.

"So, I guess punishment wasn't enough for you last time? You had to go and create a burn book to get your true feelings out?"

Welp. I guess my parents had checked their social media today after all.

I sat up and crossed my legs. "I didn't mean for it to be a burn book, Dad! It was a private blog."

He pulled out his phone. "You said Lee had no taste in

girls. That's gotta hurt. You said Mrs. Stevens wasn't a real actress. She was in *Wicked* on Broadway! And *Chicago*!"

"Her name didn't pop up on my Google search!"

"That's because she used her maiden name when she was acting. She went by Celeste Main back then."

Could I be any meaner? Could I be any more foolish? Could this get any worse?

I paced around the room.

"Dad, can I go to boarding school?"

"Nope!" he said with a shake of his head. "Listen, this is tough, but it's a good lesson for you." He leaned in close. "We raised you to be a person of integrity. That your word

is your bond. Say what you mean and mean what you say. But you have to respect others, even when you're disagreeing with them. Even when their truth and your truth may not be the same thing."

I started to feel light-headed. I took quick breaths in, panting like a dog on a hot day.

"Relax, June. I know this feels like the end of the world, but it's not."

"Ya think?"

"You can make things better."

"Nothing could make this better."

"Yes, something could: an apology."

I looked up at him. How would I even begin to apologize to all these people that I mentioned on the blog? This was bad, sure—but admitting I'd been wrong to *everyone I'd ever known* would hurt even worse. I didn't even think I'd have the courage to do it. Even with the "superpower" of being able to tell the truth no matter what.

"You can admit that you have been trying to live your truth, and that sometimes you had opinions that you didn't feel comfortable sharing. So you wrote them down, but never intended for them to be public."

I nodded. I looked forward at the floor, but my eyes weren't in focus. Dad continued, "You can admit you made a huge mistake and that you should have been less judgmental about people because everyone has flaws—but their flaws don't make them any less worthy, or less human."

"I don't know if anyone even wants to hear what I have to say anymore."

Dad looked at me. "Then you have to speak with conviction so people will have to pay attention. You'll have to do something just as impactful as the huge mistake you made in creating the blog. But in a good way. I know it's hard, but sometimes facing a challenge as difficult as this one is, is the only way to come out on the other end. And in this case, it's the only way to regain people's trust in you."

Dad gave me a kiss on the forehead and headed toward my door. "And, look, I'm not happy about what you said about your mother and me in that blog, either. But if you can apologize, I can forgive."

Dad turned his back and walked out. I knew what I had to do next.

CHAPTER TWENTY-TWO

As soon as I got to school on Tuesday, I immediately sought out Ms. West. She was the rare person I could trust to understand the horrible situation I was in, and one of the few people I said mostly nice things about in the blog.

"June, my dear," she said as I walked into the newspaper lab. "How are you?"

"I've been better," I said. "I'm sure you've heard the news."

"About you doing a great job in the school play? We were about to publish some photos of you onstage for the paper. You did great!"

"Thanks, but I don't think people really want to read about me."

I explained to her what had happened: the blog, the leak, the everything, hanging my head in shame with each detail. She looked at me with raised eyebrows, then a puzzled look, then actually let out a laugh. "I can understand why you might feel sad."

"I feel like such a fool," I said. "I feel like . . . the worst person on earth."

"I'm sure a lot of people are hurt by what you said," Ms. West said. "But you still did have your private diary leaked to the world. And I'm sure everyone has a private diary or journal or place where they share their private thoughts with the intention that they wouldn't ever be shared with anyone else. You must feel very betrayed by whoever stole it."

"Yeah," I said. "But I also feel like the most hated person at school."

"What do you think you want to do?" Ms. West asked.

"I need to apologize to everybody who's in that blog," I said. "My friends, my family, my teachers. I pretty much offended everyone I know."

"An apology is a great start," Ms. West agreed. "Do you think you're going to do this in person to each person you talked about?"

"I thought about it a lot last night, and I would like to write a column in the school newspaper, if you'll let me.

That way I can reach everyone at once and apologize with a thoughtful letter."

Ms. West sat back in her chair. "Why not publish it on your blog?"

"The last thing I want to do is attract more readers there," I said. "It's caused enough trouble. Besides, I set it back to private."

"Okay," Ms. West said. "Then a column is a great idea, June. We can save you some space for this week's issue. Can you get me a draft of whatever you want to say as soon as you can?"

"Okay," I said. "I'm not sure what I'm going to say yet."

"Just speak from the heart," Ms. West said. "Don't worry about length or editing. I'll help you with it."

I felt slightly better as Ms. West looked at me. "Cheer up, June—an apology is a step in the right direction. Get me a draft as soon as you can."

✦

After a dozen different attempts, I returned to Ms. West's office with a working version of my apology. "Wow, June," she said. "This is very brave of you to write."

"Well, it's the truth," I said.

"Okay," she said, looking over the draft. "You ready to publish this for all to see?"

"I have to apologize for what I've said about everyone."

Ms. West uploaded the story to the newspaper layout and squeezed the copy to fit in the desired spot. She typed a headline and my name to the top of the page, and then added a photograph of me from the play. I didn't know if this was going to work or not. But I had to try.

"Okay, all done. Ready to hit send?"

I looked at the computer screen. I looked at Ms. West. "It's all I've got."

I hit the return button on the keyboard, and the files were sent to the printer immediately. I took a deep breath and hoped for the best. I turned away from Ms. West and walked toward the exit.

"June," Ms. West called back. "Really, it's going to be okay."

✦

I'M SORRY

By June Jackson

My name is June Jackson, and I am truly sorry.

Many of you may have received a link to a private blog that I created that included some not-so-nice opinions about my friends, family, and neighbors. I created it because I have a big problem: I've spent my whole life telling people what I thought they wanted to hear, because I wanted to avoid potentially hurting people with my real feelings. Sometimes I even lied: small lies, exaggerations, about anything or anyone, as long as it could help me avoid the truth. Recently something in my life changed, and I've been trying to tell the truth about everything to everyone no matter what. This is very hard for me to do every day, especially when I see or believe things that others may not like or agree with. I didn't want to hurt people with my words, so I wrote down whatever feelings I thought people wouldn't like in a private blog that only I could see.

But of course, that backfired. I wrote

down things about people that were my opinions, and some of those opinions were wrong and extremely hurtful. I never meant to hurt anyone. In an effort to not hurt people's feelings, I hurt them even more by being harsher in private than I was in public.

And for that, I am truly sorry.

I'm sorry to my friends. My wonderful friends, especially my friends Nia and Lee and Olive and Alvin, who have been by my side for years. I'm sorry to my parents, who love me and care for me no matter what. I'm sorry to my teachers, who work hard every day to help us learn and study. I'm sorry to everyone in *The Wiz,* my teammates on the girls' field hockey team, to everyone at school, in Featherstone Creek, and to anyone who read my blog.

I'm sorry that I hurt your feelings. I will do whatever I can to try to make things better.

Sincerely,
June Jackson
Sixth grade

✦

It had been five days since the Leak. I'd sat through three very uncomfortable days of classes where I could feel other kids' annoyance and withering stares cutting into my skull. I tried to keep my head down and ignore it all. Nia had been out of school for the past three days, and I didn't know why—I didn't see or hear from her at all.

The paper came out on Friday. Within an hour of the start of school, my phone and emails lit up with responses and feedback on my public letter. The older the sender, the more forgiving they were.

My fellow students weren't all mean, but they weren't scrambling to become buddies with me again. Some had completely canceled me. Either way, people had the right to give me their honest feedback about what I'd done. All I could say was, "I'm sorry. You're right."

Finally, on Monday, Olive reached across the aisle during homeroom to grab my arm and said hello. "Took guts to write the column," she said. "I mean, especially knowing one of your best friends leaked your blog. I know you must feel betrayed, but you still apologized for your actions, and that means something, June."

My mouth dropped open. I looked at her. I'd been so busy writing my apology and reflecting on what I'd done that I'd completely forgotten to think about how the blog had gotten out there in the first place. A best friend had leaked my blog? Olive and Blake couldn't have leaked it because they were onstage and in the orchestra pit when it was released. As was Alvin. Lee was backstage working as crew. Chloe didn't even live in Featherstone Creek and didn't know half the people I mentioned in the blog. Plus she would never do anything to end me like that. That just left one person close to me who knew this blog existed, who lived in Featherstone Creek, and who would've been able to guess the passwords to my blog and my Instagram account. *And there was only one other person besides Chloe who knew about the truth-telling spell.* Then it hit me.

"Nia?"

"Yeah," Olive said apologetically. "I think so."

How in the world could this have happened?

"I thought for a long time about this before I decided to tell you my theory, June. I know you and Nia have had your fights, that thing about Lee, and things aren't good with you two right now. But you're not the only person she's hurt. We had our own fight a few weeks ago, and she said something really mean to me, too. Something about how no one cared about the orchestra during *The Wiz*. And this was after she told me that she's considered getting revenge on you for the whole Lee thing."

My palms grew sweaty. My face felt hot. Olive continued talking.

"That Insta post went up during the show on Sunday. You didn't have your phone then. But I saw Nia backstage.

She looked guilty, like I caught her doing something, and hurried off before I could say anything to her. She must have gotten ahold of your phone and removed the password protection on the blog and publicized the link during the second act. And then she disappeared afterward. I think Nia's the one who published your blog, June."

I remembered not finding my phone at intermission on Sunday's show. I was fishing around for it in my backpack to put up a photo from backstage on my Instagram. I only found it after the play was over. Which meant . . .

Oh. My. Goodness. Olive's theory was right.

"Could my best friend really have done this to me?" I said out loud, dazed.

I thought back to when Nia would have seen me typing in the blog, when she'd come up behind me at my locker. She must have seen it then. She also must have seen me type in my password—my middle name and the year of my birth. And even if she didn't see me type it in, this was information Nia obviously knew and could have easily guessed.

When she found out that I'd hidden the truth about Lee from her, she must have logged in and seen all the things I had written about her and everyone else. She must have decided to seek revenge.

My best friend leaked my private blog.

She humiliated me on my big night.

This is what Victoria meant by being in a pickle.

CHAPTER TWENTY-THREE

The three o'clock bell couldn't come fast enough. I dashed home from school as fast as I could, wanting to be invisible to everyone in the town.

I tried texting Nia, but she refused to respond.

JUNE: Where are you?

JUNE: Did you really?

JUNE: How in the world could you do this to me?

Where the heck was she anyway? Did she plan to take some time off for a vacation after leaking my private blog so she wouldn't have to face me?

I immediately crawled into bed when I got home. My room was a safe refuge from the public, but even in private I wanted to hide from the world. I didn't want to text, to look on social media. I didn't want to turn on my laptop, a reminder of the troublesome blog I started.

I wouldn't have started that blog had I not met Victoria in that fun house.

Before I met Victoria, my life was just fine. My little white lies here and there didn't hurt anyone *that* much. Since she'd come into my life, I'd been on punishment, I'd had a massive blowup with my best friend, and I'd had the boneheaded idea to create a diary on the *internet,* of all places, where nothing was 100 percent safe, where I wrote down the truth because I couldn't tell people what they wanted to hear, which got exposed and offended the entire town.

"My life has become a hot mess thanks to this freaking spell," I muttered under my breath. My throat and nose felt itchy. Then the air turned hazy around me. Then the haze started to swirl, and the form of a woman's body took shape again. There she was, tiara and all. Victoria.

"Hi," I said, sitting up in bed. Victoria had a soft look on her face. A look of pity.

"Hi, June," she said. "I read your column in the newspaper. That apology was really mature of you."

I mumbled a "thanks" and turned over in bed, looking down at my feet. I still thought her spell had ruined my life. But I couldn't blame Victoria for how this blog thing had gone down—I'd written all those words myself. And Nia had been the one to post it for everyone to see. That had nothing to do with Victoria.

"I'm sorry I blamed you for the leak," I said with regret. "It wasn't your fault."

"Apology accepted," she said, waving her magic wand over me. I hoped some of that fairy dust would pick me up and take me to whatever far-off land she came from so I could hide out there until this all blew over. "Things might be a hot mess right now, but that certainly wasn't my intention."

"I know," I said. "I guess I'll never get the spell lifted now, huh?"

"You've certainly made it difficult," she said. "But not impossible."

I didn't have anything more to tell the truth about at this point. And after the blog leak, no one wanted to be near me, much less talk to me. So if I wasn't going to talk to people, I didn't even have to worry about lying or telling the truth. But if I didn't have to tell the truth, how was I going to get out from under the spell?

Victoria looked at my closet, then looked at me. "June, I think you should go on the school field trip and have heart-to-heart conversations with your friends in person. Then you can tell them all what you truly think of them."

I could not think of a worse idea. "That's the last thing I want to do!" I said.

"The trip would be a great opportunity for you to try to make good with people. Think about it—you'll have an audience totally undistracted by things like cell phones and classwork. You've already written a very heartfelt piece about your mistake in the newspaper, so people will be more willing to hear you explain yourself in person and ask for their personal forgiveness again."

My head hurt thinking about it. How was I supposed to talk to every person and beg them to be my friend again? I was a social outcast! They'd never want to speak to me ever again, let alone hear my apology!

"There's no way," I said.

Victoria sat closer to me. "June, you've really struggled to understand what living truthfully under my spell really means. I want you to understand, but I also want to give you the chance to earn your freedom. So I'll give you one last task to complete in order to lift the spell."

I looked at her. What in the world would she possibly make me do now?

"Go on the camping trip and work your hardest to

ask people's forgiveness. Apologize to every single person on the trip—adults and kids—and tell them your truth to their face. If you tell the truth and work honestly to earn their forgiveness, I'll lift the spell as soon as you get back home."

Finally—Victoria had given me an actual task I could complete to end the spell, instead of just some vague "live your truth and nothing but" nonsense! But even so, I couldn't imagine sitting in the isolated woods with kids who didn't want to speak with me. Imagine Nia, with her scowl turned up toward the sky. Or Lee—what would he say to me? Or Alvin? Olive may sit next to me out of pity because she knows what happened with the leak, but I still have to beg for her forgiveness, too.

"Remember I said the truth was your superpower?" Victoria said. "Everyone's superpowers can go haywire at times. Think of this as regaining control over yours."

I thought about what would happen if I didn't go on the trip at all. Maybe everyone would talk about me behind my back. And then I'd feel like a heel if I found out all the mean things that people said about me. That would only be fair, frankly. And would make me feel even worse—especially now that I understand how hurtful it is to talk about people behind their backs. At least if I went on the trip, people would have to tell me to my face how mad they were at me.

This could also be my time to confront Nia after what happened. Okay, it was not cool for me to badmouth her behind her back. That's like cardinal rule number one of friendship. But she still stole my private diary and posted it for the entire world to see! I mean, that's a crime, right? Was what I did a crime? Did two bad deeds equal a right?

Maybe the only way to put this whole thing behind us was to have one big bad face-off over the whole thing, get it all out of our systems, and move on.

"All right," I said. Victoria was right. This was the only way I could get people to hear me out and accept my apologies. I had to take the chance. They might not all forgive me, especially not right away, but I had to try.

"Shall we start packing?" Victoria asked.

Acknowledgments

First and foremost, thanks to the team at Target for your continued support. Kate Udvari and Ann Maranzano, thank you for your partnership. And to my PRH team: Michelle Nagler, Sara Sargent, Sasha Henriques, and Joey Ho, thank you for continuing to bring this series to life. It is such a pleasure to work with all of you.

To Stephanie Smith and Brittney Bond, thank you for joining me on June's adventure. Our readers are so lucky to have both of you, and so am I.

To André Des Rochers, Bejidé Davis, and the entire Granderson Des Rochers family, thank you for your guidance through this process.

Brie Katz Waldman and Stephanie Hamada, thank

you for your support and hard work on behalf of me and the books. I appreciate your efforts so much.

Mom, Dad, Adrianne, Erica, Marcus, Lisa, and William, thank you for being my ultimate tribe. To Phoebe, Alexander, and Maxwell, thanks for all the love. I hope you adore these stories.

Thank you to my friends who are my family. To Sasha, Amelia, and Brielan, thanks for the crazy global adventures. They inspire even more books.

Finally, to my readers, I simply cannot thank you enough. Your emails, texts, posts, and DMs are so inspiring. I am so glad you love June as much as I do! Keep reading!

ABOUT THE AUTHOR AND ILLUSTRATOR

Tina Wells is the founder of RLVNT Media, a multimedia content venture serving entrepreneurs, tweens, and culturists with authentic representation. Tina has been named one of *Fast Company*'s 100 Most Creative People in Business, has been listed in *Essence*'s 40 Under 40, and has received *Cosmopolitan*'s Fun Fearless Phenom Award, among many honors. She is the author of nine books, including the bestselling tween fiction series Mackenzie Blue; its spinoff series, The Zee Files; and the marketing handbook *Chasing Youth Culture and Getting It Right*.

Brittney Bond was born in sunny South Florida to a Jamaican family. A self-taught artist, she works primarily digitally, with a passion for using appealing color palettes, intriguing lighting, and a magical and positive aura throughout her illustrations.

Check out more Honest June, available now!
Honestly, you don't want to miss it.

CHAPTER ONE

I don't know everything about life yet, but I know at least one thing is true—life's easier when you make people happy.

You want to get good grades? Tell teachers what they want to hear. Want your friends to like you? Tell them you love their clothes and their hair and their moms' cooking. Want your parents to be happy? Do what they say. Follow their rules. Happy parents equals extra dessert and cool toys and fun vacations. And, most importantly, love.

Making people happy is what I'm good at. Sometimes that means not telling people the whole truth. Or telling them no truth at all. Not because I'm trying to be mischievous! In fact, I don't like to make trouble—but it always finds me somehow. Like the time I tried to compliment my best friend Nia on a pair of shoes she was wearing. I said they made her feet look "too long." She was mad at me for a week. I vowed to say only nice things about her feet no matter what.

Or the time I accidentally knocked over the mailbox when Dad asked me to take out the trash. Instead of walking it to the corner, I put the trash bag on my old wagon to roll it down the driveway. I had the wagon aimed perfectly at the mailbox to stop its roll, but it smacked into the pole harder than I expected, knocking the mailbox over at a forty-five-degree angle. Oops! I went inside and pretended nothing happened. But the next morning, Dad was furious. His eyebrows came together in the middle of his forehead. "Stupid garbage trucks! I'm going to find out who did this and get them fired," he said. I stood there, silent. What if he found out it was me? Would he fire me as his daughter? I kept my mouth shut. He fixed the mailbox and forgot about it in a few days, thankfully.

Or the time my mother asked me if I knew what the "birds and the bees" was, and I told her the truth—"No. Should I?" This led to one of the most uncomfortable conversations of my life about boys and girls and babies and . . . *ugh!* I get the heebie-jeebies every time I think about it!

I've found in my brief eleven years on this earth that the truth isn't always necessary. Tell people what they want to hear. Smile and nod. No one gets hurt. And that is how I planned to get through the sixth grade, through middle school, and through the rest of my life.

✦

It was the Sunday of Labor Day weekend, two days before the end of summer vacation. But in Featherstone Creek, a suburb of Atlanta, the weather stays warm through fall—so it still feels just a bit like summer outside. Mom, Dad, and I got back home from our house at Lake Lanier, about an hour's drive away, late at night—just in time for me to unload my bags, eat a spoonful of peanut butter, put on my pajamas, and immediately pass out. I don't even remember if I brushed my teeth. I slept like I hadn't slept for ten years, and I didn't wake up until I heard the chime notification from Nia's text on my phone.

NIA: You there? We're coming at 5 p.m. today.

I jumped out of bed and got dressed. My best friends Nia Shorter and Olive Banks were coming over for one last summer barbecue before school started. We were going to celebrate as if it were our birthdays and New Year's

Eve combined. After tonight, we had only one more day of no homework, no teachers, no alarms to wake up to before . . . *it begins.*

"It" being our first day of the sixth grade and our first day at Featherstone Creek Middle School.

We were no longer grade-schoolers. This was middle school. Prime time. The big leagues. At FCMS, we needed to bring our A games. We needed to make a great—scratch that, *legendary*—impression from day one and live up to the legacies that our parents and grandparents had created for us. Or else our parents would be disappointed. Our neighbors wouldn't like us. Teachers wouldn't like us. Then colleges wouldn't like us. And we wouldn't get degrees. And then we wouldn't be able to get good jobs, and we'd have no money or friends or husbands, and we'd be living on our parents' couches forever, surviving on chicken wings and Flamin' Hot Cheetos. And then we'd become embarrassments to our families. If, at that point, our families still claimed us.

Okay, maybe not all these things would happen if we didn't rock middle school. I tend to overthink things sometimes . . . just part of my charm, I guess? I don't really like Cheetos anyway!

I straightened up my bedroom, which was next to Dad's office. I kept my room nice and neat so my parents wouldn't be tempted to come in and rifle through my things, like my journals or my laptop or—*gasp*—my phone.

If they thought I kept my room in order, they'd think I kept my life in order, too. I smoothed my sheets and comforter and arranged all the pillows from large to small against the headboard. I cleaned my desk and straightened my framed photos of me and Nia and me and my BFF Chloe Lawrence-Johnson, who I've known since I was a baby but who moved to Los Angeles with her family last year. I went into my bathroom and put away the bottles of leave-in conditioner and edge gel I used on my hair today to put it up into a high braided bun—my go-to hairstyle for a summertime barbecue. Tomorrow, the day before school, is wash day.

By the time I made it downstairs, my stomach was already rumbling, and my mom and dad were almost set getting food ready for the barbecue. My dad, wearing an old Howard University T-shirt and jeans, stood at the kitchen counter over a huge platter of chicken covered with barbecue sauce. My dad is a lawyer. He went to school with Nia's dad at THE Howard University, aka the Harvard of the HBCUs, aka the Mecca, according to Dad. He practically screams "H-U! You *knowwwwww*!" if anyone merely thinks about Howard in the same room as him. And he has big plans for his little girl to follow in his footsteps. Every. Single. One. He runs a law firm together with Nia's dad in downtown Featherstone Creek, with their last names on the front of their office building.

Dad wants me to either run his firm when he retires or head into politics, like Madam Vice President Kamala Harris ("H-U '86!" my dad screams at any mention of her name). I like wearing and buying nice clothes, and I definitely love MVP Harris, but I don't know how I feel about arguing with people all the time, which is what legal stuff seems to be about, at least to me. And those suits they wear in court. They're so stiff and itchy! And lady lawyers have to wear pantyhose even on hot summer days in Atlanta. Meanwhile, I get uncomfortable in jean shorts in July sometimes!

My mom is a doctor who delivers babies for all the moms in town. She works a lot, but she gets to hold babies all the time, which sounds awesome. Her family grew up in Featherstone Creek, and most of them started businesses here. Her dad, my granddad, has a family practice on Main Street. He's our family doctor and Nia's family doctor. And the doctor for half of my sixth-grade class.

My parents always mean well—they want the best for me—and I want to make them happy. Because when they're happy, the house is happy. We eat ice cream and go to the Crab Shack for dinner. And spend more time at our lake house, and my mom and I get our nails done together at the salon. And my dad laughs with his mouth wide open, and when he laughs, everyone else laughs. When my parents aren't happy, there are rain clouds, and boiled brussels sprouts for dinner, and my mom calls me by my full name—"June Naomi Jackson!"—in a high-pitched voice, and my dad's eyebrows come together on his forehead like one long, hairy caterpillar. The eyebrows scare. The. Life. Out. Of. Me.

So, if me playing field hockey, going to Howard, and being a lawyer are what's going to make them happy, then that's what I'll do. Or at least I'll *say* it's what I want to do. But a girl has a right to her own opinions. And a right to change her own opinions, too. Even if she keeps them to herself, which I am very used to doing.

✦

At 5:00 p.m. the doorbell rang. Mr. and Mrs. Shorter and Nia stood at the door. Mrs. Shorter held a large Tupperware bowl of potato salad for dinner. "Hello, June, how are you, baby? Oh, you're getting so tall," she said.

"Hi, Mrs. Shorter. My mom is in the kitchen."

"Smells good back there," Mr. Shorter said, giving me a gentle hug. Nia's parents walked toward the back of the house. Nia put an arm around me. "Girl! I thought you'd never come back!"

"We texted every day I was gone!" I said. She and Olive and I texted multiple times a day, all through summer. We basically knew where each other was at every second of the day. Nia rolled her eyes and smiled. We both giggled and ran upstairs to my bedroom. I flopped onto the bed, and Nia followed me, placing her bag down next to her.

"Sixth grade," I said. "Finally, a place where I can really express myself." I could use different-colored gel pens for my homework. Explore creative writing, join the school paper, really voice my opinions on big issues, like going vegan and saving the animals. Maybe I'd run for student body president. And I could even buy my own lunch! Freedom—I'd *literally* be able to taste it. "I'll be glad to get out from under my parents' wing," I said.

"You act as if you're going off to college," Nia said.

"They still feed you and give you an allowance." Ugh. She was *technically* right. But at least I could choose one of my own daily meals at school! That would be a taste of freedom—it had to count for something.

"Did you read the books on the summer reading list?" I asked.

"I only made it through one," Nia answered.

"Which one?"

"The shortest one. Something about the guy with the dog. It said the reading was optional."

"Optional, but encouraged," I said resolutely. I chose to read half the books on the list, though they, too, were the shortest ones. Even if teachers weren't assigning the book list as a requirement, it could only make them happy to know you did some of the reading. It might help me get in good with these teachers from the beginning. I could use all the early bonus points I could get.

A knock on the door interrupted our conversation. "It's me," Olive called out. "Sorry we're late. Mom couldn't decide what to wear. What's going on?" she asked as she opened the door, walked in, and plopped onto my bed.

"We're talking about school," I said.

"Yeah? I'm excited. Orchestra starts up again next week. I learned how to play Michael Jackson's 'Beat It' on the viola this summer."

"On to the most important topic," Nia interrupted. "What are you going to wear for the first day?"

I stood up and threw open the doors to my closet. Mom and I had gone shopping for new clothes the week before we went to Lake Lanier. She took me to the same stores where she's bought clothes for me since I was four.

"This would look so cute on you," Mom had said, holding up a pleated skirt with a printed pattern of teddy bears with their paws in honey jars. It looked like what preschoolers in the Alps might wear as part of their school wardrobe. I hated it.

I clenched my teeth. "It's cute, Mom, very cute." She tossed it into the shopping cart. I groaned internally, but I figured if I let her pick out one thing she liked, maybe I could get what I really wanted.

I wanted to go to stores that aligned more with my sense of style. This place called Fit sold women's clothes and accessories and just about every item I'd seen on some influencer or celebrity on Instagram. I pointed to a dress on a mannequin in the store window as we passed by. "I saw this dress on that dark-haired Disney Channel actress you like, and she's my age."

"Yeah, but she's an actress, playing a role. You are in sixth grade, and I don't know if I want you wearing that. It's a bit . . . mature."

"That's the point," I said. "*I'm* a bit mature now." I'm in sixth freaking grade! I am almost in a training bra! Can't she see I'm practically a *woman*?

I walked inside. There was a white sleeveless blouse

with a large bow at the neck that could pair with everything in my closet and still make me look sophisticated, even with that horrible teddy bear skirt my mom bought. But I really wanted to wear it with the pair of distressed jeans on display that had a few holes around the knees that . . . oh, look at that . . . came in my size.

She ended up buying me the blouse on the condition that I wear a sweater or jacket over it. She got her baby skirt, and I got my blouse. Everybody was happy. *Compromise.*

"So, the first day of school," Nia said. She and Olive looked at my clothes hanging neatly in my closet. "Are we doing the skinny jeans with the oversized T-shirt thing? Maybe with those Air Force 1s? Or with a shiny ballet flat? You need something that will really make a statement on the first day."

"I want something that says I'm . . . interesting," I said thoughtfully.

"Soooo, black on black on black?" Nia smirked.

"Or maybe a caftan?" Olive said.

"A caftan?" Nia asked.

"Yeah, like what my grandmother wears exclusively from April through October. She says they let her skin breathe," Olive said. "Whatever that means."

"Fashion inspiration from your grandmother may not be a good first look for the sixth grade," I said. We would have two-point-five seconds to make an impression on our fellow students and teachers at Featherstone Creek Middle School that would define how people saw us for the rest of our lives. At least that is what my dad told me about first impressions.

"Nia, what are you wearing?" Olive asked.

"Probably a skirt and my new denim jacket. Took me forever to get those rhinestones glued on, so you better believe I'm going to show off my work."

Man, why couldn't I design my own clothes, like Nia? What if I had the potential to be the next great American fashion designer like Vera Wang or Zac Posen and I'd never know it because my mom still picks out my clothes? All that potential, undiscovered. We were doing the world a disservice by not letting me pick out my own clothes!

"Girls! Food is almost ready!" my mom called from downstairs.

Nia and Olive moved toward the closet and quickly ruffled through my clothes. Nia found a white Vans T-shirt. "Pair this with that black denim skirt and you're set."

"Done," I said. "Statement made. Says 'sixth grade, here I am.' "

We gave each other high fives, then went downstairs and walked toward the back of the house for dinner.

✦

The sun was getting low in the sky, and the fireflies were just starting to make their appearance as we all gathered around the large picnic table on our patio for dinner. Olive, Nia, and I sat on the far side of the long dining table. Dad placed platters of grilled chicken and steaks in the middle of the table, along with big bowls of potato salad and fruit salad.

"Dig in, fam," Dad said. Several hands reached eagerly for the food. My mom kicked off the conversation. "Girls, are you excited for sixth grade?"

"Yes," we said in unison.

"I know that June is looking forward to field hockey," Dad said. That wasn't exactly true. *He* was excited for me to play field hockey. I had never even played before. But I went along with team tryouts because it made him happy. If I told him I didn't want to, he might think I was defying

him. And then, I'd get the eyebrows. Must. Avoid. The. Eyebrows. "Do any of you girls play sports?"

"I'm going to play basketball again this year," Nia said.

"And I'm still in dance," said Olive. "And I play viola in the orchestra."

"Wonderful," my mom responded. "June, I wished you would have taken up ballet when you were younger. It always looks good to the private schools when you have some sort of performing arts background."

"Yeah, Mom, but hard to squeeze in ballet between those field hockey practices," I said, half joking, trying to butter up my dad.

"Sixth grade," Mrs. Shorter said. "I can't believe that these babies are in sixth grade already. Where does the time go?"

"Howard's just around the corner," my dad joked. I smiled, laughing along as if I were cosigning his college prep plans. Howard's not a bad choice. But it's also not the *only* choice.

Dinner continued, with the conversation finally breaking up between the sixth graders and the adults. As the bottoms of everyone's plates became visible again, my mom announced, "Who wants cake?"

At our house, every Sunday dinner in the summertime ended with Mom's 7UP cake. It's a Southern tradition. A Jackson family tradition. A tradition I could easily skip.

The cake was a bit dense for my taste. But I didn't dare tell my mom that. Telling your mom her dessert is bad is basically telling her you don't love her. Or to never make you a cake again. I like cake. And I love my mom. So I lie.

My mother cut thick slices for my friends. They grabbed their forks and dug in. "June?"

"Yes, Mom, thank you! You know how much I love your cake!" I said. Mom placed a slice in front of me. I stabbed at the heavy slice until it turned into a mound of crumbs. I took a few bites just for show and tried not to grimace. The sugary icing wasn't too bad, though.

"How's the cake, girls?"

"Great, Mom," I said. She smiled. I smiled. *Smile and nod, June. Smile and nod.*

The adults lingered around the picnic table until the sun dipped below the tree line and darkness set in. The lightning bugs danced around our backyard with abandon, and Nia, Olive, and I skipped through the grass, laughing and singing along to our favorite songs until the parents said it was time for Nia and Olive to go.

"I don't want to say goodbye," I started to whine loudly. I felt the emotions bubble up.

"It's not goodbye, it's see you later," Olive said.

"It's 'see you in two days,' June," Nia said. "Get a grip."

We gave each other a group hug. "See you then," I said.

Dinner was over. My time to run free, laugh, dance

around, and be silly would soon be over, too. In two days I'd have to grow up, put on my game face, and become a poised young woman entering a more mature phase of her life. It was time to get serious. Sixth grade was almost here.